Grand Central:

The Untold Story

By Floyd Smith

& Rev. Benny Johnson

With Contributions from

Jackie Fells

& Kenneth Monts

Edited by Kenneth Monts

Manuscript Editing by Sister Ife Serwaa

Cover Design by Kenneth Monts

& Floyd Smith

Artwork by Ron McAdoo

Order this book online at www.trafford.com
or email orders@trafford.com

Most Trafford titles are also available at major online book retailers.

Note for Librarians: A cataloguing record for this book is available from Library
and Archives Canada at www.collectionscanada.ca/amicus/index-e.html

Printed in Victoria, BC, Canada

ISBN: 978-1-4269-1568-0

*Our mission is to efficiently provide the world's finest, most comprehensive book publishing
service, enabling every author to experience success. To find out how to publish your book, your
way, and have it available worldwide, visit us online at www.trafford.com*

Trafford rev. 8/24/2009

 **Trafford**
PUBLISHING® www.trafford.com

North America & international
toll-free: 1 888 232 4444 (USA & Canada)
phone: 250 383 6864 ♦ fax: 812 355 4082

For my mother, Ruby Jean Smith;

father, Joe Nathan Patterson;

grandmother, Annie B. Fells;

aunt, Pearlie Williams;

and uncle Benjamin Fells.

Chapter 1

The Castle

In 1896, the Supreme Court ruled in Plessy vs. Ferguson that segregation could be legally enforced so long as the facilities for blacks were equal to those for whites.

It was the spring of 1925 and a 7 year old black girl with wavy hair, kissed her mother good-bye and stepped off her front porch to walk to school. She joined her two friends who were at the corner because their parents insisted that they walked to school together. They were leaving homes which stood parallel to the railroad tracks on Jones Street near the intersection of 18thStreet. They were walking to Capitol Hill Elementary which was the school for African American children located about three-quarters of a mile to the east. Walking to school was a pleasant task. They walked past beautiful houses with manicured lawns. Most of the houses had servant quarters behind them. As they passed the intersection of 16th and Park Streets, they marveled at the massive construction from 16th Street down to 14th Street. Juanita, the little girl with the beautiful wavy hair asked her friend,

"Can you guess what they are building here?"

"Looks like a hospital," her friend answered.

"No, it's not a hospital. My father told me that it's going to be a new school for white children. And one thing for sure, we don't have to worry about going to school there," Juanita explained.

Little did Juanita know that this white school would play an important role in the civil rights and the education of African-American students. Not only would the last four of her nine children graduate from this new white school, but she would own one of the nice homes that she admired while walking to Capitol Hill Elementary school for Negro Children.

In 1954, <u>Brown v. Board of Education</u> the United States Supreme Court made the landmark decision to end the doctrine of "Separate But Equal" in public schools.

It was September of 1957 a teen-aged African American girl stepped off a city bus at 14th and Park Streets to enter Little Rock Central High School as one of the nine Negro students who were to integrate the previously all white school. As she walked toward the front door of the school in her neat, well-sewn homemade dress, a mob of whites spat at her, spewing racial slurs and screaming obscenities as they walked behind her. She continued walking, but as she walked in the door of the building, she was met by Arkansas National Guardsmen who were there to prevent her from entering the school. She turned and walked back to the bus stop where she continued to be jeered by the crowd.

With the assistance of a white woman, she was able to board the bus. While the crowd continued to torment the young female student, another group of assailants near the intersection of 16th and Park beat, kicked and threw objects at a black reporter from Memphis. The reporter, though severely hurt, picked up his hat and managed to hobble away.

Later the federal government intervened and dispatched military troops just to escort nine black students to school. These events sent rippling effects throughout the nation and the world as to how the civil rights of African Americans would be supported by the government of the United States of America.

My first memory of Little Rock Central High School was a vision that was etched in my mind not because of its historical significance, but because of its majestic stature and beauty. I can remember we had a field trip to Central High to see the Arkansas Symphony Orchestra's production of the Nutcracker Suite Ballet. Ironically, this was the first time I had ever been on a bus, considering that these yellow school buses would play an integral part of my education and the education of many other students in the Little Rock Public School District.

The year was 1970 and my name is Floyd Smith and I was 10 years old at the time. I sat next to my cousin, Jose. As children we had been raised together like brothers and we were inseparable. We had been eagerly anticipating this field trip for weeks. When the bus pulled up in front of the building of Central High School on Park Street, it seemed as if we were about to enter a huge castle. We saw a long trail leading up to that castle at the end of the "yellow brick road". The castle's front lawn was immaculate. All the trees and shrubbery were well- manicured like in a picture.

We scurried off our bus fascinated at what seemed like the trail to the gates of the Emerald City in the "Wizard of Oz". This is how we perceived this important event as 10 year old children. Finally, we made it to the front steps and walked up two more sets of steps to the huge front entrance of the castle where we looked up and saw this statue with words next to them. At the time I didn't know what it symbolized, but it was obvious to all of us that the statues and words meant something very important. It was years later before I realized what the statues truly represented. After a while, we finally made it to the front lobby and into the front hallway. The doors led straight into a huge auditorium area where the teenage castle workers got delightfully busy seating us. We got to eat our lunch in this gigantic auditorium. We were still looking around in amazement when all of a sudden; the lights dimmed down to a warm glow and very exciting music began to play. We sat wide eyed and upright in our cushiony auditorium chairs. To us, it was unbelievable how well the orchestra played. I had heard good music before because some of the members of our family were musicians, but this was good music like we'd never heard before. And the show was amazing! It held our attention then because we had never experienced this type of professional performance. While watching the ballet, which we as children had never been exposed to, we were awed by the size of this enormous auditorium. From the perspective of a fifth grader, it seemed you could fit our entire school building inside of it fifty times.

We asked our teacher, "What is this place? Is it what you called college?"

"No, she said. This is Central High School, and if you are lucky, you will go to this high school one day."

My cousin Jose and I immediately started making plans as soon as we left the show; "This is the school we want to go to. And when we make it there, we're going to be very popular. We're going to play sports, we're going to be popular with the girls and be known throughout the city!" From that day on, it was our goal to work toward going to Little

Rock Central High School. It was obvious to us even then that we were in a special place. Jose and I made each other a promise that we would not only make it to this special place, but we would also become someone special once we were there.

When we returned to our elementary school, the teacher started asking us questions about the ballet and I think my cousin and I raised our hands constantly to ask her more questions about the school. We were so excited. Jose's goal and mine was to be among the most popular students in our class at Central High. How we were going to accomplish this was easy because our grandmother always taught us how to carry ourselves in a polite and respectful manner. Grandmother always told us if you strive to be the best, people will always want to be like you or be with you. So we used that information to our advantage.

Cousin Jose and I always strove to be the best. When we did that, we always won. So, we made a lot of friends. Even the new people when they first came to school, would always come over to us and introduce themselves because we always remember what Grandmother taught us and used it to our advantage. We became real good students.

CHAPTER 2

The Big Change

A man named Neil Armstrong became the first man to walk on the moon last year. Many young males were being sent to Vietnam. The world was changing; there were defiant hippies and Black Panthers on the evening news. Most of the role models that a black kid had were sport stars such as Bob Gibson, Gale Sayers and Lew Alcindor. With the exception of sports, not many black faces were seen on TV. Robert Kennedy and Martin Luther King Jr. were recently assassinated and many large cities experienced riots. Curtis Mayfield still reminded us that "We're A Winner" and we're moving on up and James Brown said "Say It Loud, I'm Black and I'm Proud." Black was beautiful, the Afro hair style was hip and we all did the funky penguin and the funky chicken at the dance parties. It was something special to be black.

Little Juanita is in her early fifties, married, and has nine children. She teaches at Arkansas School for the Blind and her 6th child Ernest will be graduating from Central High in about a year. Within three years Juanita, with her husband and family, would be living in a home in the shadows of Central High about 50 yards from the south side of the building.

It was 1970 at Gibbs elementary. This was the year that the school district really started to transfer black kids and white kids; busing them out to different schools in an attempt to maintain a racial balance. This balance was to provide all races with an equal education.

In our previous years, we didn't know anything about the Little Rock Nine or the court case of Brown Vs. The Topeka Board of Education. We were just kids in elementary school having the time of our lives. We didn't know that the books we were reading were of poorer condition than the ones the white kids were reading in their school. The bona fide news came at the end of the year to Gibbs elementary; what we'd heard all year since the fourth grade was just that they were going to start splitting up the schools. They were going to start busing black kids to white schools and white kids to black schools. We thought we were getting a raw deal being bused away from our friends and families. But we didn't have any say so in the way the school was going to be run. Like I said previously, the schools we were going to were all black with no white students. Well, in my neighborhood, we had some white people. When we first moved there, we had some white kids that we would play with. But after a while, the family packed up and moved away to another neighborhood. Our white friends didn't last too long. If one would move, we'd look across the street and yet another family would be gone. And so on and so on pretty much, until we looked up one day and our whole neighborhood looked majority black.

So in the 4th grade Jose and I were still at Gibbs elementary. We would play basketball and we would win all the time. We would play baseball and always win. It was the same thing with football. He or I would either be the running back or the receiver and we would always win. So everybody, our peers, looked up to us and began to admire us as talented guys. I can remember how my cousin Jose was kind of the ladies man. He was a good athlete also, but there was this one little girl he used to like a lot. Since they were in the same room, if she got out of class to go to the restroom or get a drink of water, he would ask to be excused right after her in order to turn the knob on the fountain so she could drink. She wouldn't even have to turn her own faucet. He would do that for her on a regular basis. Every time I came out of the restroom, I would see them outside together. Everybody wanted to be a friend of mine and my cousin's. We were in the same grade. We had a sixth grade at Gibbs, but the sixth graders at that time had already begun to be bused.

Chapter 3

Introduction to Integration

Remember that we, as children, didn't know anything about the Little Rock Nine back then or what they did. There weren't any significant desegregated schools until 1970 or 1971. From my perspective, that was the first time. Even though we had the 1957 crisis of Central High School, the real desegregation started in 1970 and 1971 in Little Rock. Yes, there were a few schools with both white and black students, but the percentages were not equal. The exceptions were a few elementary schools in bi-cultural neighborhoods in some areas of Little Rock. So going into the year that they were supposed to bus children, they did not do it in the elementary schools that year. The plan was that busing would begin in elementary schools the following year. We were only in the fourth grade at that time. We had enough going on making it to the next year, our last year in elementary school, not knowing what to expect. When we came back to school the next year, they bused my cousin Jackie, who was in the sixth grade, to a different school. My brothers and the rest of the kids in my family had been bused to different schools during their Middle School and Jr. High School years. Jose and I went back to the fifth grade, which would be our last year together at the elementary school level.

We decided that since this was going to be our last year, we were going to do some things there to make it our best year ever in elementary. We decided that we wanted to be safety patrols. We were already fire marshals for the fourth grade level. So we thought that safety patrol belts would also make us look nice to the little girls. It seemed like the girls were catching our eye more and more, and safety patrol men garnered plenty of respect.

During fifth grade registration, the parents would bring their children to the school and into the cafeteria. That's where the registration processing was done. All the parents would go and sit down at the specified grade level and register their children. My mother and my aunt did that for Jose and me. We were 10 or so going on 11 and we decided that this would be our year to shine since the six graders were being bused already to another school.

So school begins. I remember the principal came up and got me and Jose and took us to her office. She said that she wanted us to be safety patrols. At the time, we were some of the most popular guys at our level. Jose would "play it off" by helping girls, opening the doors for teachers etc. He was that type of guy. The principal would drop something and he would run and pick it up and hand it to her. So, I started doing the same thing right behind him because that is also what I had been taught. Our good behavior continued and the principal decided she wanted young men like us to be safety patrol. She gave us our safety patrol supplies and we loved it! We had an orange belt with a shiny badge on it and a long pole with a wavering flag on the end. When a kid walked up to a corner, they would have to wait until we proudly stuck out those poles. Jose was on one side, I was on the other corner across the street. All the cars would stop for the kids to walk across, and then we would let our poles up for the car to go on about their way.

By about the end of the week, we had gotten into the groove. I can remember the principal came by there one day and we were really doing our thing trying to impress her. But later on, this one little girl suddenly appeared out of nowhere. She was running trying to catch up with some of her friends. A car was coming up fast on the horizon. Boosted with pride and excitement, although Jose and I were about fifteen or twenty yards away from the girl, we immediately stuck out our poles for the car to "halt". The car slammed on its brakes. You could hear the screeching noise everywhere and maybe a couple of words from the driver we weren't allowed to say. The driver barely stopped just in time where he was almost touching our flag. But we let the little girl run on down the street to the smell of burnt rubber.

The principal came running out of her office. I had never seen an older lady run that fast. She said, "You two come here now! Come here now to my office!" We sheepishly followed her to her office where she took our safety patrol belts and our poles from us. She told us that our services were no longer needed and that she was going to have to find someone else. Well, this really hurt our feelings. We knew we had done wrong, but we had done all right up until that last Friday of the first week. We were just kids; 10 or 11 yrs old at that time, left alone and unsupervised. But, anyway we had gotten fired, I guess you could say, and were devastated because now we're just ordinary students at an elementary school.

Jose and I played football and baseball; just doing our thing on the playground like the other kids. However, we were still the two most popular guys in the fifth grade. We ate our lunch and ran outside just to play with the others because it seemed like the recess time would come and go so fast.

We're finally down to the end of our fifth grade year at Gibbs elementary and we're very glad. By now, we all know what Middle School we we're going to attend. My brothers and cousins all went to or had gone to Southwest Middle School. That would also be the school that we would attend. We had heard that they have a football team at Southwest for the 7th graders and we knew that was what we wanted to do. Jose and I had said we were going to play basketball and football. And I was also going to run track, so when we get to Southwest Middle; they had better look out for us.

We graduated together from Gibbs elementary at the end of the school year, but my cousin Jose's, who was my best friend, parents decided that they would move to Detroit, Michigan. Sadly, he and I would not be attending the next school level together. I was the only member in my entire family except Jose who was the same age or even the same approximate grade level. Wherever I went to school, now, I would be on my own since Jose would be moving with his family to Michigan that summer. This was a painful life lesson to know that now; I was kind of alone on my own.

It's the end of the year and we are preparing to go to school again. We would not be going just to an all black school anymore. The school we will be attending would be mixed: 50% black and 50% white. This will be my first year going to school with white students. Even though this was the first year of full integration, the schools were still segregated socially. The two races still stayed mostly to themselves. The school that I attended previously, most people called it the neighborhood school and everybody knew each other in the neighborhood school.

All the black people were still segregated pretty much, but there are so many black kids at the new school that I don't know. And as far as the white students are concerned, I not only did I not know any of them; but I really didn't know what to say to them or even how to approach them.

The white children are also just as curious as we are about what is going on. I have never met most of the black kids at this new school before and I don't know any of the white students because they are all from different parts of town. So not only did we, as black kids have to get used to the white students, but we also have to get to know the new black students that we had never seen before. Every morning when we'd first arrive to school, all the mothers would drop their children off and all the kids would meet in the cafeteria. From there we would just go outside and play. Everybody would meet and try to get to know each other.

I remember an incident a couple of times when we were having lunch. This one little white boy wanted to slap box. He would always come up to one of the black children on the playground and only ask them to slap box. My mother and grandmother had always warned me to stay away from these types of situations. So when he came up to me, I said no. He then asked to slap box with one of my friends when we were on the playground. My friend took him on and tagged him so bad; it was kind of embarrassing to me. He wasn't really fighting him, but he was just slapping him, like the game it was. Where I grew up, if you couldn't fight back, you either "stayed out the heat" so to speak, or you would get picked on. This was a little white boy who obviously didn't know the rule, so I had turned him down. Finally, I said ok, I think just to save him the embarrassment from my friend. I went on and slapped at him. He would try to swing at me and I would block his punches every time. He took both of his hands and whacked. I took both of my hands and whack, whack.

We were slap boxing and I was just quicker than he was. He dropped to the ground and gave up. When he got up though, I was surprised that he wanted to do it again. Something was wrong. When he got up again, the same thing happened; whack, whack, whack. This time, he hit the ground and his face turned red. From that point on, he was embarrassed because this made him look weak. As long as I was letting him win, he was strong and aggressive proving that he was better than the black kids. I turned that against him by just being more aggressive than he was.

After that, he didn't try to slap box with any other black children. He was aspiring to be a school bully like his brother before him, but he only bullied the white kids from that point on. He never dealt with us black kids again. I remember hearing years later that only the strongest Africans had survived during slavery, but we black kids then also had pride and confidence.

Anyway, during the middle school year of the 6th grade, we were obtaining new black friends as well as new white friends. Some whites would talk to you, but for the most part they didn't talk to the blacks. Well, in all fairness, we didn't know each other; so it was pretty much just watching, waiting, and gawking at each other. It was a very awkward situation. No one really knew how to introduce themselves or what to say to each other. As the year went on we found out that white kids weren't any different than we were. We were all just kids, neither one of us knowing what was going on or why all of a sudden we were thrown together going to the same schools. White kids seemed more aware growing up that they went to a different school than we did and we black kids knew that for some reason, we did not go to school with them. But, the next year, a change dropped out of the sky and here we all are at the same school. It would be months and in some cases years before we finally learned how to relate to each other. We had to learn how to like and respect each other.

It was coming down to the football tryouts at Southwest Middle School, but the six graders weren't allowed to play yet. Only the 7th graders could play. I knew this was the rule, but I secretly tried out anyway, and made the team. I was first string flanker for the Ponies! We had two teams; the Mustangs and The Ponies. So in the 6th grade I was starting with 7th graders and I thought that was the greatest thing until it came down to the day before we were going to play a game. I was placed as a second stringer, but another flanker who was a 7th grader who wanted to play went and told the coach that I was only in the 6th grade. I remember the coach walked briskly up to me and said "Floyd, what grade are you in? Are you only in the 6th grade?" I admitted, "Yes sir. I am." "Go turn in your uniform", was all that he said. It really upset me because I had such big plans. My plans still were to be a BMOC (Big Man On Campus), a great athlete, and make it to Central High School and become famous. This was a terrible set back because I wasn't allowed to play football in the 6th grade. Well, I had made the team though, even though I couldn't play. I understood why… So… those were the rules.

We would catch the school bus every day at 20th and Marshall. It got to the place where our bus stop became the most famous in the area. We felt like the bus we were on was the most popular one in the area because all of our neighborhood friends rode it. We had it going on. I remember that we were pretty rough on the bus drivers at the time. One bus driver in particular who was a minister, we called "Rebber". A lot of the kids would throw stuff at him when his back was turned. They would always throw paper and junk just to mess with him, not to really hit him. They started throwing trash out the window at cars or whatever. Some kids were always doing something mischievous on his bus.

One day Rebber got completely fed up with us and threatened to drive us to the police station and drop us off. He drove us straight to the police station, but we did become afraid and wouldn't get off the bus. The police talked to him and he finally drove us on back home.

The next day, we had a new driver. It was a lady and she had her ways. She had heard about what used to go on with our bus and she was a mean, no-nonsense lady. She gave us assigned seats. She would not let the boys sit right behind her. All of the boy's seats were on side of the bus where the door opened up. Their seats could not be behind any drivers anymore like they used to be. Only the girls were now allowed to sit on her side. Anyway, when we got too noisy and didn't do what she told us to do, she would deliberately hit a bump head on and make us jump up in our seats –"I told you all to be quiet, didn't I!?" Or she would turn a corner and hit a curb real fast in a way that would upset us and make us bounce all back in our seats. She had her ways. They had finally found a bus driver with a knowledge of children and a keen sense of aerodynamics who could handle us.

Kids got wild at the end of the last day of school. We ran to the lockers, which we had never had before and we would throw papers, books and articles of clothing all over the floor. Black kids would throw their stuff at the white kids they didn't like and white kids would throw stuff at the black kids they didn't like. That's how it went. If there was someone you didn't like, you threw stuff at them on the last day at the end of the school year or you fought them. That's about how my first year of integration ended in my sixth grade year.

CHAPTER 4

Tiger Spirit

Richard Nixon resigned as president of the United States under shame for his involvement in the Watergate scandals. Our troops have been called home from Vietnam. Marvin Gaye sang protest songs. Gerald Ford became president of the country. The country was preparing for its grandest birthday of all- the bicentennial celebration in 1976. Marijuana use is very popular among many teens and young adults and the sound of disco is dominating the airwaves. The Camelot and the Robot were the popular dances. A smiling peanut farmer from Georgia named Jimmy Carter won the Democratic nomination and was later elected our new president.

The year was 1975 and I was attending Paul Lawrence Dunbar Junior High. Dunbar was located about a half mile east of Central High. For many years, up until 1955, Dunbar had been a high school for Black students. It was built two years after the completion of Little Rock Senior High School, which was now renamed Central. Dunbar remained the high school for Black students until Horace Mann High School was completed in 1955.

Paul Lawrence Dunbar's 440 yard relay times, judging from the national sports magazine, was second best in the nation. We were one of the top 2 track teams in the country. There we were; Dunbar was the top Track and Cross Country programs in the state. A time ago, I had essentially vowed to be one of the top athletes in the school. I worked for a work program called the EOA {Equal Opportunity Association}. It was a summer work program that Federal government had for the teenagers during the summer. In the morning I would go to work. I had gotten a much appreciated job then cleaning the inside of the school buses. When I got off work, I would go home and prepare to go to one of the track meets in North Little Rock, which was just across the Arkansas River. I wasn't the best then, but I got one of the better times in the state. I had qualified to go to the nationals even though I don't think that's going to happen. The nationals are out of state and my parents don't have enough money to send me out of state to a national track meet and I don't make enough money either.

OK, it's getting close to August when we will have to go to Central High and take our physicals for the athletic teams. I felt like I was in good shape, but all the football players; old football players, new football players, were all taking their physicals down at Central's football stadium. Everybody in the Little Rock School District had to take their physicals at the same place. All kinds of doctors and nurses were there; heart doctors, head doctors, butt doctors and it was very hot. We would wake up in the morning, go to practice, go home, and then we'd eat something at the house and take a nap. By the time you'd take a nap though, it was time to go back to school for practice. So, I would get on up and go back to school for a full day's practice. This routine would last for three weeks. In three weeks, the coach would get you into pretty good shape.

We had learned most of the plays, so by now we are ready to play ball. While we practice, the High Steppers, Central High's famous girl drill team, and all the cheerleaders are further up practicing on the field.

The band is also practicing. This is a different atmosphere from both Dunbar and Southwest. The band and cheerleaders did not practice anywhere in sight. We're really getting the feel of being at Central now; up at the big school as we called it. I was beginning to feel the history and tradition of a great school. Something special was in the air here. I was being introduced to the SPIRIT OF THE TIGER!!!

It really seemed more like a privilege than an opportunity to be able to play here at the "big school". I am getting very much into the spirit now and I know what I need to do to claim my position. We're out there on the field where the coaches would have us to sit up in alphabetical order; where you could just kind of hang out up there and get to see all the new incoming girls. And it's fun, you know, because it's a much bigger experience than I am used to, and there's a lot more people at this school. It is a very interesting new year.

It was time for school to start. Two-a-day practices are over with. We are just going to school and having only one practice a day. I have not made it to the varsity team yet because I am too young, but I plan on making a name for myself anyway. One of the coaches saw me playing and liked what they saw. I am learning more and more about the magnetic spirit of the Central High Tigers. Everybody is involved; the student body, the cheerleaders, the team. I mean this is the school where everybody is pulling for you.

I play for the tenth grade team now, and I am one of the best defenders. Coach Boone could play me anywhere. He played me at linebacker, and he'd play me on defensive tackle. He would place me wherever he needed me and I would always play my heart out. I just wanted to play my role of being on a winning team. This season is going to be over with soon. We're getting close to the end of the year, but we see some good things. We have a lot of enthusiastic tenth graders who are going to be around to learn, so the coach has much to build on.

This is the first year at Central -my sophomore year. Like I said, going to school at Central is cool. The halls are jammed packed and I mean jammed up. When you hear the bell ring, it's just like you're in New York Grand Central station in the excitement of a busy crowd headed somewhere. If you don't know where you are going, you are going to be late for class because it's just that packed. You had to figure out a way to run to the restroom, get your books and get to class before the bell rings. You only have 5 minutes and sometimes it feels like you need 50. So what you have to do is take enough books for 2 or 3 classes so that when the bell rings, you can run to the rest room and then run on to the next class. These teachers here have a rule that you must be in your seat when the bell rings or you are considered late. If you are still standing when that bell rings, some of them will mark you as tardy. So, in spite of all the terrific energy in the school, I discover that the teachers are really strict here at Central.

Our Principal's name was Mr. Morris Holmes. I met and had a few conversations with him and he knew my older brothers. I thought he was the best principal in the world. He related to the students very well, maybe because he had children that were our age. He is real personable with everybody.

Mr. Holmes continually asked that we help keep the school clean. He would come over the intercom and ask that if we saw papers and trash, to please pick it up. Don't rely on someone else to pick it up, he would say, when you can be the one to pick it up and throw it away. To me he was an excellent role model for all of us because he was a good leader and he taught us all to be leaders.

He would always talk to you when he saw you in the hallway. If he saw you running late, he would get behind you and encourage you along so you would make it to your next class on time. He was a great man who gave me a lot of encouraging words and made everyone feel special at that school. I am very proud to have had him as my principal. He made me feel that I could achieve anything at Central if I put my mind to it.

Football season came to a close and we football players learn to start lifting weights during basketball season which is off-season for us. All the football players also attend the basketball games. We started this little play where we meet right under the goal. We called ourselves the "sixth man" and we would try to distract the opposing team away from making a free throw. Aw yes, we were in with the in-crowd.

We supported our basketball team; they supported our football team. Everybody was going to all the games to support each other. I would even go to the gymnastic meets in spite of the fact that the young ladies would wear those skin-tight little uniforms. We were a close school. I mean some of the white guys that I first met during the integration project in the 6th and 7th grade are some of my best friends now because we really got to know each other.

CHAPTER 5

The Big Question

Now that we are older, the white students and the Black students can talk to each other much better now as young men. When we first met several years ago, we were confused about how to relate to each other. We didn't know what to say or how to talk to each other about anything. They would stare at me and I would stare at them like we were aliens from different planets. I wasn't used to any white friends since my earliest childhood. I remember being hurt and confused when the parents of my little white friends moved them away from me. Then the other one lived several blocks away; too far away according to my mother's concern, so all my friends were African American. So now is my time to ask if desegregation worked?

Yes. If they hadn't decided to force integration by busing us years ago against the wishes of many parents- both white and black who were set in the old ways, black and white children would never have made friends with each other like they are now. I wouldn't have met a good true friend like John Bates and some other friends I played sports with who happened to be white. I would never have met these guys and we would never have gotten to know each other. I mean these are some good guys. We learned that we could count on each other. We didn't hang out at each other houses a lot. I am sure that it was probably still their parents "hang ups". But I'm sure that in and out of school, we are friends. So, yes I can say that I made some new friends who happen to be called "white" and I believe they feel the same way about me. This is what went on for me at Central High. Now as far as statewide; during some of my travel in this state, I can say we still have a long way to go.

Back at Central, we'll see how it goes next year. Maybe by our 11th grade year we can do better and win the championship. Track season came up and we had a good track team. During my AAU Sprinter campaign, I hadn't been beaten yet in the 100 and 200 meters. We got some guys that make pretty good time, though, so I feel also like I should just wait and make myself a better football player. My goal this year was to be the sprinter champ, but now, in my tenth grade year, I'd better just let these older guys do it because they are pretty fast. Even though I did beat a couple of them in the AAU, these guys are older and wiry. So I decided that I should sit back and learn how to do a long jump and participate in the field events.

Coach Clyde Horton is teaching and also became a good buddy. Coach Horton was the premiere track coach in the whole state. He fielded a great squad every year dating back to the sixties. He was a very likable person with a great sense of humor. He made us laugh all the time which took away the stress and he related to us very well. He is the one who inspired me with the techniques you need to learn in order to do a good long jump. My first long jump was at the 19 foot mark and it is not good enough to compete. This is my first time doing a long jump, but I think I can learn to be better. For one thing, he told me to concentrate on the furthest mark I wanted to hit. My goal now is to spend extra time with him learning how to do something that I didn't do quite as well.

I take art under Ms. Anthony. This is something else I love to do here at Central. So at age fifteen, I thought that maybe I would be an art major. He gave us very challenging art work to do. In study hall I would finish my math and other difficult homework first, and then I would practice on my sketches. One day, while I was looking at my study hall teacher and doing my sketches, I decided to do a sketch of him. I would try to look at him and making sure he didn't notice as I went along, then sketch some more. The last time I looked up at him, here he was, standing beside me and looking over my shoulder. He calmly asked me what I was doing. I just handed him the entire sketch pad showing him the almost finished picture of himself. He said, "Oh! You're an artist and a pretty good one." I proudly thanked him and he asked to keep the sketch of himself.

I discovered that he is the drama teacher. He continued to stand beside me, and then asked me to take up drama as one of my classes next year. I can take drama class and become a stage manager. He told me what a stage manager does and it seemed easy enough. I made A's in P.E. I made A's in art and now, I see another class I might be able to make an A in. This way I can keep my GPA up while I play sports. I told him yes, just because I thought I might be able to make an A in it. I'd had my eye out for some classes that I could make an A in and found one. In English and in math, I had to really work on these. Even though I can do it, these two things I worked at, but never got an A in, so I'm happy to accept the drama class and become a stage manager.

I told my friend Tony and my cousin Jackie that I was going to be a drama stage manager. They were surprised, but I told them that the teacher wanted me in it and I think I can make an A in it. They decided to get in the drama class too. I didn't know anything about any drama stage manager, but I'm glad I found out about it because it helped me understand what goes on behind the scenes of stage productions.

CHAPTER 6

The Unfair Shadow

It was time to graduate from my tenth grade year. We say goodbye to the "old" guys, but are secretly joyful that there's going to have to be some young bloods stepping up and I'm going to be one of them.

Coach moved me during spring training from safety to defensive corner. So that will be interesting because I am going to be a star at cornerback which is one of the two positions played on the defense side on a football team. I took it on because I had played safety over at Southwest in the 7th grade.

We were practicing hard and running hard. Coach Boone is teaching us how to reduce our open field tackle. When we thought we were at the limit of our endurance, he would ask for a little more. Tony got moved to the corner back position when he had previously played safety on the right side behind me. Jackie is at safety and Harold got moved to a safety position. Jerry Noble is a receiver and he moved to a corner. Keith Curry, Bruce McDaniel and some of the guys I've been playing with; a lot of my friends are playing in the defensive back positions.

Jackie, little Bud Jerry Noble and I started doing a lot of running. We would run all the way up from either our homes or Central to the War Memorial and back because our dreams are to get scholarships to college by playing sports. We hear about it all the time, you know, athletes who win scholarships to college and become famous. We know that we can play and we're going to make sure we're ready to win. We would also run AAU track (Amateur Athletic Union). It is the Junior Track And Field Olympics during summer months.

Although it wasn't my specialty, I did manage to come back on the AAU championship.

But, we are teenaged young men who also need to work to make money to buy our own clothes for the school year. Most of us do all we can to give our parents money for the household and help pay bills at home. A lot of kids at Central are in the same situation, so I don't think anything about that and my limited time. We just do what we have to do and hope someone will notice me and offer me a scholarship to college. That is the reason I worked so hard to be a good athlete.

After seeing the movie "Enter the Dragon", I also took Tae Kwan Do for the training. I loved the martial arts, but I am in it for the training, not because I like to fight. I never liked to fight anyone, but I guess I day dreamed about the part about discipline and concentration and all. I personally entered the tournament only because my karate instructor asked me to and it is excellent training. We learned to do 200 pushups!

So here I am I participating in football, track and field, basketball, a little karate and keeping my grades up. If I didn't keep my grades up, I wouldn't be allowed to participate in extracurricular activities at home or at school.

I learned a lot about Central that year. We had a losing season when we should have won. I had some disagreements about some of the players who were out there on the field and the ones who were placed on the bench. A couple of the men on the bench were consistently better than some of the ones on the field. If you have your best men waiting on the bench, how do you plan on winning? Well, thankfully, the season was over.

We spent the summer less enthusiastically training for the upcoming year. This is my 11th grade year and the coach has picked me out as a star at the defensive corner. As usual, we go up to the school for registration where we see all these new girls coming in that we'd like to impress. I still feel pretty good about our team this year. We should do quite well especially if we can play good defense. My cousin Jackie, Harold Noble, Tony Downs, Bruce McDaniel and Jerry Noble were the rotation in the defensive backfield. The lineup that I think is the best could be a winner only if the coach plays it that way.

It was the first week of school in our 11th grade year. I got my math class, 6th period P.E and I got the 5th period study hall. Most athletes got 5th period study hall because for practical training purposes, all athletes got 6th period Physical Education class. We are now up for our first game at Central this year. I am a starter for the first time. I'm excited because the position is easy to me. It's the position I started off playing- defensive back. So, everything is working out just fine. I can see my future now. My future is playing defensive back, not wide receiver. They run my way and I make the tackle. I'm doing what I'm supposed to do at my position.

I was going after the ball the first time they threw it and I had a disagreement with the referee. The ball was up for grabs, so I went for it, but he called pass interference on me. This was my first varsity game and when this happened, my immediate reaction was, Oh, Come on! Hold on! Why did you call that against me? I wouldn't say I was a disgruntled player, but I was definitely upset about the unfairness. The coach quietly walked up to me and said, "Floyd, don't worry about it." Coach Boone said, "You know what not to do next time. It will be alright. Watch and see." That calmed me down and we won this game.

The next game was in Pine Bluff. Whoa! I'll never forget this game. Pine Bluff had a lightning fast running back, but we felt like we could stop him, or at least contain him. This was not so easy. It's not so easy playing on the opponent's home turf for the first time and hearing their crowd booing you. I guess I was a sensitive lad and it gave me a weird feeling in the pit of my stomach. I'll admit that I got kind of dizzy-like, you know. So that running back came running my way and at the split second, he made quick cut to the left and I fell down. He was able to run the ball back for 40 or fifty yards. Oh no! This is not supposed to happen. Not to me. He's not supposed to be able to do that to me. But, then, he did it again! I almost got him the last time. I had my hands on him; but Pine Bluff ended up winning that game with the support of their fans.

The long ride home on the bus was quiet and somber. No one was talking to each other. It's no fun going home on a losing bus, but I learned from this. We'd win a game, you lose a game. You'd lose a game, we win a game. And that's how it is. However, what makes the feeling of losing worse is because I still believe we have better players sitting on the bench than we have out in the field. So, if this doesn't change, I realize that I will have to play better than I am in order for our team to win. This is my first year playing defensive back, but I'm one of the better tacklers on the team. I am the 2nd leading tackler that Central has. When my friends are around; Teddy Morris and Joe McCraney, I am able to tackle even better with them in place.

Finally, I remember, at the end of the season, we only had three games left to play. We went to Hot Springs and I will never forget that game either. They ran all over us like they owned us just like that running back in Pine Bluff. I'm making my tackles. Teddy ended up with about 16 tackles and I ended up with 13. Some of the other players' heads weren't in the game that day. I don't want to mention any names because some of them are still friends of mine, but they weren't doing their share and we had better players sitting on the bench.

When that game was over and we returned home, coach Faison told me I would have to fight for my position this week. Why should I have to fight for my position? Everyone knows that I am the second leading tackler.

We had to play our biggest cross-town rival next which was Little Rock Hall High. I knew most of the Hall players and many of them were my friends. If Central had a home game and Hall played on Thursday, they would come to our games and sit at a certain area. We had a designated area at each other's school where we would sit. Both schools would come on their off day and watch the other team play.

Anyway, now I have to fight for my position. The coach put this other guy who wasn't as fast as I was in my position. He was a senior, but he couldn't tackle as well as I could. I finally told the coach that the guy was not as good as I am. He told me, "We are trying to help him get a scholarship." Well, the reason I thought you practiced so hard was so you could play the best and that's how you won a scholarship. You are supposed to put your best out there on the field and I knew I was the best.

So the coach and I were not seeing eye-to-eye now. I walked away angry, definitely a disgruntled player. Then he moved me to the bench. After doing my part to win, playing as a team player and being one of the top tacklers on the team, this is how they reward me by sitting me on the bench. I was very upset and it was a low point when I realized they apparently placed him because of the color of his skin. I have not heard of this being done for a black player to get a scholarship before. Maybe it happened before I came or it might be happening now, but that was an extremely low point in my career. I had worked hard and gave 100%. I had practiced hard all summer long for my position. For them to just give it to someone who was not as good of a player as me just wasn't right.

I was angry and hurt because I had been betrayed like this. So, I decided not to play football for Central anymore. This was a major decision for me and more than spite, or just a pout, or whatever. We were continuing to lose and the coach still played this same player in my position. Now at the end of the season when my skills are at peak and while other players continue to make mistakes that I don't make, I am not being allowed to play.

So, I'm demoralized. On my last time watching the game while sitting on the bench, my mind started to wander. Since we are losing anyway, I could be sitting up in the stands with my other friends or a girl and having some fun. Oh boy! Well, coach, you don't need me to play..., well I won't play.

It's funny that when things are in disarray, rumors start to fly or at least you start to notice them more anyway. But I like to keep things based on facts. One of the managers told us that some of our players got letters from colleges, but weren't notified of the tryouts. We also heard a rumor that the coach dumped some player's recruiting letters in the trash. I'm not sure if this was true. They may not have notified them of a tryout, but I think a recruiting letter would also have gone to his house.

We desperately wanted to get scholarships to college and play sports. That was our goal. I would go home and think about how to accomplish this night and day. That had become my life. In fact, the only way I see I'm going to be able to get to college at this point is through a scholarship. My parents can't send me to college. Sometimes we are barely making ends meet at home. For my parents to try to take money away from everyone else in order to send me to college was not possible. I wouldn't even ask them to make that kind of sacrifice. I was betrayed after working hard and now I couldn't have a good game. One bad game after many good games and I'm placed on the bench as if I'm one of the worst players? It upset me too much especially since all my friends would see this when we were playing Hall High. So, Jackie and I both left the field.

We began to notice that the majority of the players being played now are white. It was glaringly obviously to us and we started discussing this black and white thing. Some of us were walking across the field one day. We had gotten about half way to the steps when we looked up and saw Coach Cox walking behind us. I don't know to this day if he had been walking behind us all along in order to talk to us or what. I don't know if he knew how he was going to talk to me after doing what he did. I didn't know if it was his move or the defense coach's move to bench us or really what all was going on. He continued walking behind us with his head to the side and never did say anything at all. Finally, he turned and went his way and we went ours.

CHAPTER 7

Redeem Yourself

I was embarrassed that rumor got out all over town that Floyd Smith was not going to be playing ball anymore for Central. I lived on 19th and Marshall. Some people called it 19th High and it was the cutoff line to go to Hall High School. I already had a friend named Benny Johnson who stayed in the same neighborhood and went to Hall high. He found out about my situation and from there the not so secret got out at Hall. People at Hall were happy though. They persuaded me to come over there to play. They thought if I came to Hall, they could be the state champions maybe in football, basketball or field and track. I had to persuade my mother though, that this was the best thing to do. She was never into sports anyway and said she had sent all her children to Central. Her first and final decision was that I had to stay at Central because she had sent my older brothers there and they knew our family. She didn't care if I was out of football because I could get hurt out there anyway.

My stomach got tight at the thought of having to play another year like the one I had been through; with some of the players on the bench being better than the ones on the field. So then, I would listen to my mother completely. I would be sitting in the stands watching the game when I wanted. That's just what I wanted to do.

Our football season is over and one of my teachers started talking to me about staying there and believing in maintaining my football career at Central. Coach Crater had talked to him. He said Coach Crater told him if I came back the next year, I would make All State. He reassured me how good a football player I was. But you know what, coach Crater never did talk to me about that-Not once. At that time he had never discussed with me why I was pushed out or whether I was good, bad or indifferent, so I didn't know if I could believe that was really coming from him. All I had wanted to do was play ball and go to college on a scholarship.

Then a coach called me at home from Parkview. "Come on here and we will play your best at Parkview, if that's what you want." I felt like a lottery ticket.

When I would leave out of my classes, I started noticing that there would be Coach Crater around or about. It happened over and over again and I started wondering if he was teaching a class in the main building. This went on for a few weeks. He found out that I liked this particular teacher and that he and I had a close relationship.

In the meantime, my good friends kept disagreeing with me, saying, "Oh man don't go anywhere", like it was nothing. "Just wait. We don't want you to leave." It was kind of sad. Even today, I think how wrong it was that my feelings were messed around like that as a kid who was just trying to play football.

Well, the bottom line was that I wasn't going anywhere because my mother had said I couldn't go anywhere else. My thing now was that I just wasn't going to play. I didn't get a chance to play football the rest of the year against Parkview or Hall high and we lost both of those games. If I had played, would we have won? I don't know, but I knew we would have had a better chance of winning. So, the next time I picked up on Coach Crater deliberately avoiding me, I told him that I wanted to play, but it was under conditions. I really spoke up this time because he knew he could lose me permanently. I told him what I knew about the defense and why he had better players on the bench than in the field.

I worked it hard, hard. We worked it hard! Every time coach blew the whistle, I was the first one up or the first one down. I started noticing other men trying to tackle like me. They would maneuver and run like me. I noticed this and I'm proud. I didn't consider myself as being a leader, but someone had to speak up finally against what was going on. One day, one of the local T.V. stations commentators came and asked me about our defense. I simply explained that Central's defense was quite intact with the exception of one player. I let them know that I thought Tony Downs should be a starter on defense. I had let the coaches know that I thought Tony should be a starter on defense because he was better than the other player in that position.

So we work hard and can feel the team unity. I can see the team unity. We got a good running back and a good quarterback. Danny Nutt is going to be our starting quarterback for next year. We have a whole crew of good running backs. We have a good team even if we aren't so sure about how good our defense plays. Coach Boone trained us to where we are the top secondary team in the entire state. It's going to be a great season this school year after all because the whole football team worked out all summer long. We knew that we were ready and in shape to defeat the other football teams. It's going to be a great season the next year after all..., and I never had any more problems.

CHAPTER 8

Dancin' Ain't No Sport!

Mr. Deaton, the drama teacher had a problem. He was working on this theatrical production called Bye Bye Birdy and he didn't have enough actors. We had signed up to be stage managers, not actors. We would move things around and furnish the stage for the dramas, but he was now threatening to flunk us all if we didn't participate in his play. There goes my A, I thought, but I'm not an actor. We participated and did everything else he asked us to do as stage managers, now he's threatening to flunk us because we don't want to act and dance?

"I'm no dancer, sir, I'm a football player." I remember telling him. "That is how we are planning on getting scholarships to college." He became angry and started calling us the gladiators: "In the Roman days, you'd be in the stadium surrounded by people hollering kill, kill, kill." I say, "Naw, we're not killing or anything like that. You haven't watched a game in a long, long time." We all laughed about that.

This goes on for days and into weeks. It got crucial though when he called me and Tony in to meet him in his drama room and warned us; "If you all are not going to participate in this play, I'm going to flunk you all!" Mr. Deaton forced Jackie, and Tony and myself to be in the play or we would get an F" on our report card. He then picked up a key chain and threw it at Jackie. It was funny because the chain missed

Jackie and Jackie picked it up and threw it back at him. Poor man, he was doing everything he could to get us in this play. Seeing that he was so bent out of shape over it and he really could give us an F, we finally decided to be in his stupid ol' play.

He excitedly gave us our parts to play and we had to learn the script quickly. We learned to do this silly little dance that he had seen somewhere or made up. Then he brought in the girls. We got to dance with these girls. Well, now it's getting to be fun. We had no idea that we would be dancing with females. I was thinking all the time ballet, tight tights and jumping around through the air. But we got to practice picking girls up around their waist and holding them close, so it's fun now. I'm glad I joined. We start really getting into this play and it's not nearly as bad as we thought it would be. We helped build the set, paint it just the right color and did whatever else we needed to do for a successful play.

I guess we practiced on stage for about a month for this play: BYE BYE BIRDY. I think Mr. Deaton was really brilliant at being a producer. He brought some stuff out of me that I didn't know I had because I never had to use this kind of creativity before. That may be part of the reason I later decided to write a book. Being friends with him was a good thing because he was excellent at what he did. Being friends with him also helped me to be successful in my own little private music production.

I remember back to when I was in the study hall class; he would wear some pretty expensive jewelry. I had just come back from a karate tournament in which I won first place. One of the teachers wanted me to bring the trophy up to the front of the class so he could take a picture. Mr. Deaton saw my trophy and said, "Wait a minute." He then gave me his jewelry to hold in the picture and smiled at me with pride. One piece of quartz jewelry he said was a thousand years old or something. I don't really remember now. He was a peculiar man and apparently he had a lot of money. He didn't seem to care what they said about him when he would fight for things that normal people wouldn't fight for.

I remember we had holes in our curtains where they had dry rotted for quite a while. Mr. Deaton had asked the school several times for some new ones, so he called the news people there. When they arrived, he stuck his head through one of the big holes in the curtains and greeted them. They took his picture like this and put it in the newspaper. Some of the things he fought for, people would laugh at him and he was a very funny guy.

We laughed for weeks about that one, but boy was the school district was mad at him. During that time they would call him down stairs constantly to come to the main office. Our stage manager class had a tow rope. One of the little white guys climbed out there on the rope from the very top window and we swung this kid on the rope all around the building. Someone from the neighborhood called in and told how we had a kid hanging outside on a rope who was going to get killed.

We heard Mr. Deaton rushing back up the stairs and we quickly snatched the little boy back in and hid the rope. We hid the rope up in this catwalk. When he came in rushing everyone was in their seat reading or writing and acting like nothing was going on. He rushed in huffing and puffing and fussing, throwing his keychain around. He was even funnier to us when he was mad.

Anyway, we're kids and we got a big kick out of doing him like that. Every time he'd leave, we'd hang another kid out there on a rope and swing him across the building. A neighbor would call the school and Mr. Dean would rush back up the stairs fussing. It was hilarious. We did it a couple of more times before he found the rope and hid it from us.

Anyway that was one of the crazy things we used to do in our stage managing class. That year I got an A in gym, an A in stage management, and an A in art. I had been successful in keeping my GPA up a lot higher than was necessary. I learned this method from one of my older friends in the neighborhood who went by the name of Shakey. He told me to always take a class you're sure you can get an A in, in order to keep your GPA up. And that's how you do it.

It was in the spring of my 11th grade year that the district is planning a big talent show. Mr. Anthony is doing a poster. Mr. Anthony, my art teacher always did a poster for the Students Black Culture (SBC) Talent Show. Shakey and Mitch and Al asked me to be a dancer with the team, but I am not a dancer. I'm not going to even say what happened on that, but I did not dance on any talent show. Anyway the talent show is coming up and Mr. Anthony asked me, "Who is doing all that dancing?" "The 20th Street Dancers, I said. That's my neighborhood dance group." He said, "Do you know Shakey?" I said, "Oh yes. Shakey is in the 20th Street Dance Group."

That's what he did when he made the poster advertising for the talent show. Mr. Anthony wrote that one of the groups on the talent show would be Shakey and the 20th Street Dancers. He gave Shakey and his group top billing. Shakey didn't have anything to do with putting his name first on the poster. I know this is true because I was there when Mr. Anthony made the poster. Putting Shakey's name in front of The 20ᵗʰ Street Dancers was just a promotional move. Mr. Anthony advertised the thing like he was going to bring Shakey out because everybody in town at that time knew him. They would always show up to come and see Shakey dance. He asked me a little bit more about him. I told him how Shakey had this little move he called the "broke leg" that was wild.

Anyway, this caused some conflict between Mitch and Shakey because when Mitch saw the poster, he thought Shake had written the names down like that with his name first. Shakey didn't understand how it happened and told Mitch that he didn't know anything about it and had nothing to do with that poster.

I know he had no part in it. We all lived in the same neighborhood for a long time. These 20ᵗʰ Street Dancers were the first group like them in Little Rock who would meet and do the Camelot and the Robot and those dances back then. They set a whole new trend. I remember that night they did a talent show up at Dunbar Center when they struck their pose. They opened the curtains and the first person everybody saw was Shakey, then Mitch and then Al. The people went crazy at how they had their pants cut and the way they were dressed. That's when their reputation started. They were so good that the lady who was playing the record got too excited jumping around and accidentally kicked the cord off the machine. They didn't even get a chance to finish their choreography, but the crowd went wild over these "dancing fools". Shakey would always leap off the stage when it came time for him to do his solo; but they had started together and were always a group.

That was the history I gave Mr. Anthony about the 20th Street Dancers. He put a star by Shakey's name anyway. It was a great looking poster, but Mitch got rightfully mad, and refused to perform. The tickets had already been sold out, so some of the sponsors some kind of way, talked Mitch into going on and doing the show because he had been more than unhappy about it. There was also a dancing group called Pretty Tight coming from Parkview High that was supposed to be very good, but our 20th Street Dancers were the group of the evening.

We were getting down to the week of the talent show and everybody was excited. We worked out the scheme for me as a stage manager to do the lighting for 20th Street. They use blinking lights at the beginning of their performances or sometimes at the end, and that's what they asked me to do. Mr. Deaton will never go for that though -uh uh. I'm thinking to myself, "Even though performers do it all over town, he doesn't like blinking those lights." So 20th Street asked me to fade the lights. I said, "OK then. I can do that. I'm going to give it to you!"

All the other acts go through their routines, dancing, singing, etc. Then the Twentieth Street Dancers came on stage. As soon as I heard them announced, I blinked the lights and the crowd went wild. I mean the crowd was going crazy over the 20th Street Dancers. I decided to continue blinking the lights until I heard Mr. Deaton come running up there. "Don't do the lights like that, don't do that. You're going to blow this place up!" So I stopped. By this time I see Shakey has jumped off the stage. He jumped off the stage and began to do this "broke leg" dancing routine and the crowd is going wild, stomping and cheering. Mitch tried to call Shakey back to the stage because he was taking too much of the music away down there dancing by himself, but he could not hear him. Meanwhile, like I say, the crowd is going crazy. So I tell one of the other stage hands to close that door and lock it when Mr. Deaton goes out. Don't let him back in until I get through with this routine. As soon as Mr. Deaton left, I started back blinking those lights. Mr. Edwards, who was playing the music said, "That group that was dancing out there put on quite a show." I was proud that they were my neighborhood dance group.

Anyway, other groups kept coming up and asking me to do their lights just like that; but I only did it once for the 20th Street Dancers. For some reason, the judges gave 20th Street 3rd place. Mitch got mad. Mitch had a temper anyway. He wanted the golden trophy because he felt that after the problem he went through and the way the crowd was going on, they were the best act. I would say so too. That's not how it worked out though. They were the grown judges and they were in control of who won or who lost.

We're moving on getting close to the end of the 11th grade year. On Fridays, we had a tradition where everybody could dress up if they wanted to. This one time at lunchtime, my good buddies, Teddy, Jackie and I were on first floor south center in front of the stairs when I heard somebody say, "Floyd, look up". I looked upstairs and saw Teddy standing there with a trash can full of water. I moved out of the way. Another student came back too slow. He was looking real clean that day. He had worn a nice suit and had pick combed his hair out in a smooth Afro. He looked like he was going to a church convention. Teddy poured that water out and it went all over him.

Although that happened years ago when I was a kid at Central, to this day, every time I pass those stairs, I can't help but to look up. Then it's still hard for me to stop laughing when I remember what happened there.

CHAPTER 9

Back to Business

In the spring of 1978 we started back to our usual spring training. We lifted weights and ran in order to get in shape for our senior year. This year, I think we looked real good; like we could go on and win the state championship. We have some young football players coming to Central from Dunbar Junior High. They are unusually big guys for their age that will be able to fill in and help out. The senior guys got together and met with the whole team. Together we made a commitment that we weren't going away for the summer and get all out of shape then come back in the fall and quickly try to get back in shape for the football season. We all enrolled in a nautilus weight program up at the university. Everyone made a commitment that over the summer we were going to lift weights and come back in even better shape because this year, we are going to win the state football title.

Spring training ended and the summer began. For the past three years, I have been running the AAU track during the summer because I lift weights during spring training. We all enrolled in a fitness program to get ready for football season and also I had been getting my exercise for the AAU, which is the Summer Track and Field Junior Olympic. This made me more all around physically fit. Track events increase your endurance and flexibility. I did the long jump event for Central and

I was a sprinter in my senior year. I was the sprinter champion for the 100 yard dash. Like I said previously, we qualified to go to the nationals, but we are an independent league that has to have their own boarding expense once we got there.

My mother is a personal duty nurse, my stepfather works for the sanitation department, and I have younger brothers and sisters. My parents aren't able to give me the necessary money for lodging that the trip requires. As it would happen, this summer I ended up winning the regional sprinter championship in the 200 relay, but I would never see any other national competition. She doesn't have the necessary money for me to travel just to go run. Those are the breaks in sports competitions.

All summer long I rode my 10-speed bicycle out to nautilus early in the morning. I had gotten my weight program discounted with a special deal with the school. I sped from 19th and Marshall to 12th and University. There I would do weight training by lifting and pressing. Then I would ride back to home to Central, run the bleachers and then turn around and run the track. I would work out using a routine like this 7 days a week. I was determined because I had made my mind up years ago in grammar school to be the best. By now I knew that it took more than enough to be the best. It's hard to describe how you can feel yourself becoming stronger and faster because that "edge" kind of sneaks up on you. In about a month, I felt the difference and was proud at how some people looked at me. I was in "tip-top" condition.

During the workouts, I would always check on my other team members to see if they were following up on what we had agreed upon. So far, everybody who participated in the agreement is working out also. Everybody is committed to winning and for sure, I'm doing my part. I go to the weight room whether I feel like it or not just as we promised each other we would do. I continued this ruthless training week in, week out, and my speed timing has really increased. So, I'm feeling great physically and great about the upcoming football season.

I still have to work at one of the banks downtown cleaning up after hours. And I have to save my money to help my parents buy school clothes. I also want to save enough money to go see my relatives in Detroit who I miss very much since they moved away from Little Rock. Therefore, before school starts back, I would like to spend a week in Detroit with my aunt, uncle and my favorite cousin Jose.

I'm down to the last few weeks of working out with the nautilus. I have to lock up my bicycle because my younger brother liked to take it on long rides and it wouldn't be there when I needed it. This last week he had hidden my lock so that he would be able to ride at his leisure when I wasn't there to catch him. This particular time, I went on to my work out without the lock for my bike.

Lo and behold! I saw this guy riding away down University on my bike just as I was coming out of the gym. I had to walk from University Avenue to 19th and Marshal, looking for my bicycle all the way. I had not said anything before and shared with him, but this time I let my parents know that I had had enough of having to walk because of my little brother. Thereafter I would have to jog to the nautilus center and wait forever for a bus to take me home. It was miserable. However, I had made a commitment and fortunately, I managed to finish the week out before it was time to visit my relatives in Detroit.

CHAPTER 10

A Detroit Perspective

It was a long ride up to Detroit, Michigan on the Greyhound bus. It took at least 24 hours, not to mention the few extra stops in little towns and rest areas. But it was a good experience for me. It was the first time I had taken such a long journey by myself. It gave me time to think and plan while I looked out the window at this big country. The first stop outside of Arkansas was Nashville, Tennessee where we stopped over for about an hour or so. I didn't know what I was expecting, but the landscape to me appeared very similar to Arkansas until we got to Chicago. The bus stopped over in Chicago for about three hours and I had the opportunity to see the downtown area for the first time. It was huge, sophisticated cluttered and very crowded compared to downtown Little Rock. After that, we stopped in Toledo, Ohio for about 30 minutes or so. I was drifting off to sleep and before I knew it, I was in Detroit looking at my laughing uncle and my cousin Jose again, who came to pick me up.

I spent a week with them in Detroit. The people appeared rougher to me. This was the first time I had ever seen gangs which was a very different and unpleasant experience. The police would detain and interview you if they saw too many young people together. I had to adjust to that. My cousin told me to be careful where I went because if you go somewhere you don't know, you could get into a fight just because you were in a different neighborhood. It was an unusual experience for me in Detroit then than in Little Rock. That's about all I can say about that. Anyway, I made it back to Little Rock in one piece in time to register for school and begin our spring training.

CHAPTER 11

I'm a yellow fellow

We returned to school around the middle of August and immediately began training. Everybody on the team had come back in excellent shape. The offense was looking good and so was the defense. We were going to be the team to beat. We had not been rated to be the winning team, but we knew down in our hearts that we could win this time and we were going to do it! We beat our first team easily. So easy, it was like a professional team against a low-rated high school team. That is when we knew for sure our summer commitment had paid off. The giant had awakened.

I guess it was around this time that I first fell in love. It was about the first week of school when I saw this yellow dress. She was the prettiest young lady in a yellow dress walking with a friend of mine across the street. I asked my friend about this certain girl and she told me her name and agreed to inconspicuously introduce me to her. I was able to chat with this special girl and ask her out on a date. After that, every morning, Tony, Jerry, and I would walk to school real early. She would meet me in the area around the picnic table every morning about the same time. Tammy had agreed to be my girlfriend.

From that point on, Tammy and I connected and dated all through the football season. I became very fond of Tammy and would meet her at lunch time and every chance I could. We rode the bus together. The vice principal asked me to be a hall monitor and it gave me an opportunity to be with her. One day he found us hidden by the ROTC area, talking and hugging each other- just what most teenagers did at that time. I respected her and she respected me, so nothing else would occur then.

Anyway, back to what was going on at the school at that time. Some of the cheerleaders would get toilet tissue and target certain football player's houses. They would sometimes do pranks like this to all the popular football players and cheerleaders homes and they decided to get me one night. However, they got my aunt's house instead. She stayed right next door to us and one of them must have seen me over there one day and thought it was my house. They threw toilet tissue all over her trees and made it look like a toilet tissued Christmas tree.

A lot of that went on though, but mostly we would do that to opposing team members and their friend's homes. We would sneak over at night while everyone was asleep. However, for some reason, some of the cheer leaders decided they would do mine for fun. We were in good spirits. Winning had made life grand. Being on a winning team made the school year pass quickly and everybody agreed that we had "out matched them" this year.

Before a big game, we would have pep assemblies. Man, being on stage and having the whole student body cheer you on was fantastic. And when they called your name: FLOYD SMITH! Then they would say- Go win! I felt like I was on top of the world. It was an outstanding school and I felt like all of us were real close. The Blacks, Whites, Mexicans and or whoever went to the school sincerely cared about and supported each other. Not only were we committed to winning, but wherever we played, our student body would also come and cheer us on. We had become a successful school on the playing field and off. We had made Central High School a pleasant atmosphere for all races and a model for the nation as to how integration could take us into becoming successful as a diverse society.

CHAPTER 12

It's Hard to Be Humble When You're A Senior

So far, everything I had dreamed about as a fifth grader and all the plans I had made in attending Central High School were coming true. We were winning all our games. Wherever our team would play, at whatever school, there would be a sell out crowd. At a couple of schools where we played, we were amazed that the rival team's student body had come early and were waiting outside for our bus to arrive. They didn't want anything but just to get a look at us. Some of them were waving at us and made us feel like we were famous stars. So, everything is looking very good, just like I planned.

When it was time for the homecoming game, we had to walk the Homecoming Queen down the court. We had just finished a good practice when we found out that most of the guys had chosen their own girlfriends to put on the list for homecoming Queen. They are not going to vote for the popular girl that students think should win. They brought me a copy of the list and I discovered that a very good and friendly student named Geraldine was not on it. Tony and I took the list and said some of these girl's names need to go and Geraldine's name must be on this list. She is a very nice, friendly and intelligent young lady, and we think she should be our queen. So, we replaced one name on the list with hers and submitted it for homecoming queen. The student body can choose from the other list of contestants.

We went on and played homecoming and sure enough, we had made the right decision. We clapped and cheered because Geraldine did win for Homecoming Queen. After the game, there was a dance at the gym. I was very disappointed that Tammy's parents wouldn't let her go out that night and I had to go to the Homecoming dance without her. The drama department had the gym all dressed up and decorated spectacular. It didn't even look like the same place. When you first walked into the door, you walked through vapors from dry ice evaporating behind the doors. I went on inside without a date where everybody was having a good time. I remember asking this one girl to dance, but she said "No, because you are dating Tammy". I said, "Yes, but all I asked you for was a dance." She laughed a bit and finally got up and we danced and danced. After that I got a chance to dance with several dressed up young ladies. By the end of the night, I was tired, though. It had ended up being a highly successful day and a fun night after all.

Next, we will have to play Parkview and Hall High before we go out of town and play Fort Smith. We started practicing to beat Fort Smith first. We looked at the film of their plays and started planning our strategical tactics early because we know they are tough. Fort Smith High School has a major reputation. They throw a lot and have a highly decent running back.

When the bus got to Fort Smith, just like most of our games now, students were already standing outside waiting to smoke us over because we have a smokin' reputation. Central High is ranked as the number one team to beat. Not only that, but to every school we go now, Central always draws a huge crowd.

Well, I enjoyed the competition and liked the atmosphere of the school, but we ended up beating them pretty badly. What was strange about this, though, is that even after the game was over, the crowd did not leave. Even though I was happy, I felt a sense of their disappointment. But still, the students didn't leave and go home.

I looked over to the fence where a bunch of girls were cheering me and calling me over to them. Tony walked over to the fence with me. The girls jumped up on top of the fence and asked me to raise my hand to them because they wanted to touch me for good luck! Coach Cox was watching though, and he strolled over to the fence. He seemed amused, but he made us stop all the fun by telling them that we had to get ready to go home, *now!,* and get back on the bus. Anyway, we touched the girls and told them we had been very glad to meet them also. We went back to the locker room, dressed, and returned to our own school where Central High School Tigers are still undefeated.

Parkview was our next to the last game that year. We played a real tough game with them. So far, we have dominated Parkview. In the beginning of this game, we had scored six points against them. However, at the end of the game, we broke out for a touchdown and one of Parkview's defenses picked the ball up and ran and made a touchdown. The game ended up being a tie. We don't feel too bad though, because a tie means Central still remains undefeated.

We are now preparing for our Turkey Day game, which is played annually on Thanksgiving Day. This is one of the most popular games Central played against Hall High. It was known as the Bell Bowl Game against Hall High. The Student Body (the whole school) made a huge bonfire to spirit the preparation for the Hall High game. A group of our players gathered a bunch of wood and whatever other stuff we could burn. That was our pep rally. Later on we would eat a lot of turkey and which ever team won this game would win the State football title.

The second game was played to a crowd with standing room only. Alumni who had attended high school years ago returned to see this game. It was pretty much like a love fest and if you didn't get there early, you didn't get a seat. So, we are prepared to play this second day game. We made it up to Hall High School with everybody feeling good and playing hard. If we don't beat Hall, we will not win the state championship. Hall has a real good running back and good players. In addition, some of my old friends from Dunbar Jr. High play for Hall. The running back came my way and I stopped him. The quarter back came my way and I managed to stop him also. So far, we are doing very well. Therefore, Hall makes an adjustment. They have a hidden secret by running up the middle away from where I was playing. I slide into the mud around half time and I heard my shoulder pop out of place! Has what mom warned me about come true?

Dr. Smith ran onto the field and looked at my shoulder. He gave me some smelling salts or something. He decided I was able to continue to play only if I wanted to, but to stop immediately if it hurt too bad. It was the final half of the last game for the championship in my senior year. Did I want to continue to play? Is water wet?

In the final part of the game, Hall High started passing. A guy I recognized from elementary school named Ralph had caught a couple of passes from off the side of my defense. They started rapidly moving the ball and got a touchdown. After that, where ever Ralph went, I went with him and tackled him relentlessly. It was brother Earl, though who brought him down and knocked him out of the game. The next time the quarterback threw the ball; we picked it off and made a touchdown.

I'll never forget how we won that game just barely at a score of 16-14; but we ended up winning The State Championship that year. All the student body rushed out onto the field and went crazy; even from Hall High. And the girls! They just dived all over us! I didn't even feel any pain; until the next day I felt like I'd been hit by a truck.

One of our most revered traditions was- before and after every game was to say a prayer right out there in the middle of the field for the teams and the student body. This would be my last football game playing at Central so I was ecstatic that we, Central High with Floyd Smith, had won the championship. Everybody left after our prayer and went to eat some Thanksgiving turkey. I left with a friend of mine and I was starting to feel the burn too much, so we set up a date that we, Tammy, and all our close friends could go out somewhere for dinner. Turkey day is over with, but I couldn't sleep right away thinking about the All States team and something else.

CHAPTER 13

Floyd Smith Wasn't There

We returned to school from the Thanksgiving Holiday. That prior Sunday the All States team was announced in the newspaper. We are walking to school. Tony, Noble and I are going to meet one of the defense coaches. What was strange today is that he had never come out in front of the school to meet us there before. He asked if I had read the paper and did I agree with who all had made All State this year. He asked me hesitantly if I agreed with it. He was fumbling. I said, "My name wasn't on there? "

Coach Carter had promised to me the All State if I came back to play and won this year, and he knew it. I replied that since we are the *State Champions*, my name and everybody on our team should be on All States list. I told him it had been very important to me to get All States list and I had worked very hard for it. As a matter of fact, I had set my career plans on it to go on to college. My mother had gone back to school and gotten her GED to become a nurse's aide last year to help me, but my stepfather didn't make enough money to send me to college. It was necessary for me to win a scholarship or I would have to go to work somewhere right after High School in order to make money. I was speechless and didn't know if I wanted to yell or cry. Could it be possible after all that someone really thought I wasn't good enough?

Everybody at Central cares about each other, it seems; at least the students do. You would have to have attended Central to understand our family style camaraderie. One of my friends was a white female. If I missed class, she would loan me her notes to take home and study and I would do the same thing for her. If she wasn't at class, I would save my notes for her. That's how we cared about each other. Everybody wanted to make sure that if you were a senior, you had what you needed to graduate with good grades. It was the same with the basketball team. They would be in the stands routing for us when we played football and the football players would go to basketball games and rout for them. This betrayal on the part of the teaching staff was strange and very upsetting. I had the grades, I had the skills. I would see some who weren't as smart as I was going on to college. Like they say, life's not fair.

Life was getting more hectic. My daily routine was that I had to be at home by a certain time. Once I left football practice, I had to check in with my mother before I could go to karate practice. Once I finished that, if she still had to work, I would go to her and spend the night at her client's house if necessary. That's what I had to do. I had four younger brothers and sisters in the house until my stepfather got home. If she had to stay long at a patient's house, she would cook and leave it on the stove. It was my responsibility to make sure that they ate and did their chores. I, as the oldest still at home had to keep the house and yard clean and also help discipline and guide my young siblings. I know a lot of students have to do this, but for a teenager, it is quite a responsibility. I couldn't come up short and I was on a strict time frame then or I could wind up on punishment by not being allowed to go see my friends, talk on the phone and what not.

My girlfriend Tammy would call me some days and I couldn't be there for her. This particular weekend, I had to run some errands and wasn't there again when she called. It upset my mother when she called several times because she had to work nights sometimes and would be trying to get some rest. She told me she was tired of answering my phone calls. This was before we had cell phones, so I talked to Tammy about it and arranged to talk to her when it would not wake her up- only at certain times. She didn't understand that I could talk to her only when it was convenient for me. She got mad and broke up with me, sadly because she didn't understand all the responsibilities I honestly had to do. She felt like it was because I was away with other females. I didn't want to break up with her, but she told me I made her feel like a fool by calling and calling and not being there for her. I tried to explain that I didn't want her to look like a fool, without saying that I had plans of really being there for her. But, I lost my best girlfriend and maybe wife, anyway. I had loved talking to her on and off through out the day. Now that would end.

My senior year had been great up to this point. When I had to break up with Tammy, I asked to date another girl at Central, but she started running. Or at least I felt she was running from me because of Tammy. I had dated a girl at another school before that, but it didn't feel right. So, I stopped trying for a while and that's how I ended up with nobody for prom.

CHAPTER 14

Deadlines

The school year is going on. The most enjoyment would be walking with friends to school in the morning, and then going to my homeroom. This year I wasn't able to have Mr. Anthony for my art teacher, so I was hoping that someone would discover my artwork. Maybe I could get a scholarship that way. In homeroom, the teacher would spend about 15 or 20 minutes taking roll call. There are several Smiths in homeroom. Several of them I group up with at the same table are fun young ladies. We tell jokes to each other and talk about some of the important things in our lives.

Sometimes the teacher would sit there and listen. Unlike today, we never disrespected him with bad language and he never disrespected us kids. One day he called me, "Floyd, he said. I heard you didn't get a scholarship in football, but I personally think you could go to the Ohio State University and play football up there." He said "Floyd, where do you want a scholarship?" I froze. Could this be true? It was shocking to me that he had said Ohio State University because this is the school I had often thought about playing for. Not knowing anything else to say, I agreed with him- "Ohio State University."

I think he probably had overheard me talking in homeroom with my friends about what I wanted to do after high school and how we were going to do great things with our lives, etc. He said I had one week to give him a decision, but I knew it was going to be hard to convince my mother to let me go that far away from home. I waited several days to ask her just right, but as predicted she said, "No, and why couldn't I find someplace closer to home than Ohio?" It was always what if this happens, what if that happens and you're away from your people and you're going to need more money to live etc.etc ....

It came down to the last day of the one week and I was desperate. I had to by-pass her some kind of way. I knew she wouldn't like it, but I asked my grandmother about going. I explained to big mother that I really wanted to go and I had an opportunity for a 4 year scholarship but my mother had to sign for it. My grandmother agreed and tried to convince her, but my mother refused to have me that far away from home. I had to turn it down because she wanted me to go to college, but I felt she was nervous about not having me around. I was angry and hurt that she didn't really understand, but she had the last word this time even over my grandmother. I had to tell my homeroom teacher that my mother wouldn't allow me to go. I had to respect my parent's decisions.

CHAPTER 15

Being A Champion

We have a few months left before track season started. We had all been working out at Harding College in Searcy where the indoor track meet was to be held. The coach put me in the 800-meter relay and the long jump. I never asked why, I just tried my best to do it. The long jump was now my best activity. I jumped 21'11". I was proud of this because I worked on long jumping for years and had finally gotten very good at it. I was satisfied. We won the 800 meter heat, but I did not win the race. I came in third. I remember I pulled a hamstring and it sure did hurt, so I told the coach that I couldn't run long distance anymore. I much preferred sprints. But even in the sprints, as hard as I tried, the pulled hamstring just wouldn't let me stretch out fast enough anymore. Jerry and Ed were placed to run 2nd leg of the relays.

I understood that I couldn't run in long distance, but I thought I would be ready for the sprint. I over-heard Jerry and Ed telling the coach that they had always been the fastest anyway. That encouraged me to prove myself even more. We were preparing for the battle for state championship in track, so I said why don't I run next to Jerry and Ed and see how much slower I am than they are. Coach placed us in a practice race next to each other and I beat both of them. He decided to switch our racing positions. Determined to win, I ran the relay anyway with a sore hamstring. I told the coach that for four years, I had done well on the track here, but I was becoming disappointed with it because I never had the money to go to the finals anyway. I ran the 100 yards & a couple of days later- the 200. The coach said "Floyd, you're ready even if you did pull a hamstring. The last guy had run 21 seconds flat on the relay which is very fast on 800 meter relay team. I told him, "Coach I have been practicing this for years, but I'm sorry I can't do it now because I have pulled my hamstring." A part of me didn't want to do it anymore anyway because of the past disappointments, but I had proven to myself that I could. So that last year we won our conference, then won the state and were again on our way to the championships.

One of our team mates had a big lead in the last race, and then he dropped the baton. We were real disappointed about this. We had won the State Championship, but were thereafter disqualified to proceed to the National Championships. We ended up getting second place with one of the best times ever, though. That's how our track team ended up my last year in high school. Football season is over with, track season is over with and it is the end of my senior high school year.

I know that we've come a long way since 6th grade at Bale/Southwest Middle School. We were among the original poster children for the positive results of diversity in education at work. As I reflect on race relationships at Central High School, it seems as if integration is paying off and we are on track for bigger and better things.

CHAPTER 16

The Future Appears To Be Bright.

It is late spring of 1979 and we are getting ready for the big senior prom. Tammy had broken up with me and didn't return. I wasn't dating anyone and I was looking for a lady to take to the prom. I told my friends that I didn't have a date because of this and I didn't want to attend our last prom alone. One day, one of the girls in my homeroom named Debra came up to me and said she didn't have a date either and she would love to be my date. She would go with me.

I picked a tuxedo and Deb already had a nice dress. We really weren't matched up or anything exciting. I had picked out my tux the day before the prom. It was a deep maroon color with a ruffled shirt and a cummerbund. The jacket had small tails- not the full tails that went almost to the floor, but the shorter ones that came down just below the back of the thighs. I had also bought the latest styled shiny, black patent-leather shoes. Debra wore a powder blue full length formal gown which was graceful and pretty. Like I said, we weren't well matched in our dress, but Deb had a good attitude about it and our personalities matched up well with each other.

My brother had just bought a new Cadillac and he had a friend from Florida named Dre. Dre was a basketball star at the University of

Arkansas at Little Rock (UALR). My brother's friend chauffeured us because I didn't have a driver's license yet. My friend Shake had said he couldn't go to the prom either because his brother had wrecked their car. I surprised him when I told him that we had a chauffeur- driven Cadillac and he could double date with us.

After Dre picked me up, we went and picked up Shakey and then Cheryl first. Then we picked up Debra and did all the senior ball formalities of taking each others pictures being sophisticated and cool while putting on the ladies corsages. Then we slowly cruised to the Barton Coliseum in a brand new, green and white Cadillac.

Dre drove us right to the front door of the hall where our prom was held. There was a long line of beautiful people entering the Coliseum and it was great. Everyone was wondering who was in the Cadillac. My brother's friend had worn all white just for us. Dre wore a white suit jacket with no shirt, white slacks, white shoes and a white driving cap, and he was about 6 feet 5 inches tall. He stretched out of the Cadillac and opened the door for us while everyone was watching as if we were movie stars for this one night in our young lives.

Some of them started clapping and cheered when we went inside the ball and met with all our friends and our team mates sitting together at the same table. We took a lot of pictures, ate a lot of hors d'oeuvre, and danced to the band a while. We had a wonderful time and before we knew it, it was all over and time for us to go home. Dre had arrived to pick us up. We dropped off Shake and Cheryl, and then we had to drop Debra off at her Grandmothers. We got a chance to talk and talk about our future plans, though. I thanked her for the evening; kissed her and walked her inside. It was real nice. We were happy, and that is how my senior prom ended- too soon.

Now it is time to graduate. We all have to take the final semester exams and I was more than a little worried. I had not studied well because of the pressures on me from the last semester. I had slacked off with my homework using what extra time I had left during the day for extracurricular activities. Now I was forced to play catch up. I sweated it out in the exam room and graduated well only because my grades had been high for the first three quarters. But one thing I learned, for sure. You don't do well trying to catch up by depending on other people's notes.

Graduation day has finally arrived. We rehearsed the graduation ceremony and the march walk. We went through it about three times to get it just right. Graduating from high school is a major move. You are moving away from the old and familiar to a completely different world. I mean some of these people you've known all these years, you will never see again in life. That evening, our family members arrived and we all stood together in the hallway waiting for the cue for us to march.

We were all excited and tension is in the air. Along with the excitement is some sadness, however. The strange feeling of loss also hits you. Then you realize that a lot of these people you have been going to school with all of your life will be moving on and you don't know when or if you will ever see them again. Many of my good friends went away to college in other states. Some of them went off to work somewhere else. Some of them married people we didn't know and moved away. Many of my fellow classmates have been attending school with me since the 1st grade and I met many more of them in the 6th grade when the district first integrated our schools.

As I stood there and looked around it appeared that the integration of our schools had worked out well. There had been many ups and downs, but it appeared to me overall, in my own eyes, that attending school with other ethnicities was a positive endeavor and I am proud to be a part of this graduating class. I listened to the speeches of four my classmates and they explained the significance of the four Greek statures that I gazed upon when I was an elementary school student on a field trip to this wonderful school with the building that looked to me at the time like a castle. The statures represented Ambition, Personality, Opportunity and Preparation. I may not have gotten everything that this school provided but those four qualities were indeed instilled in my life and I was optimistic that it would help me to succeed in whatever my future panned out to be. So this was it- the final chapter in my young school career. It hit me then that just like when Jose left to live in Detroit; I was facing life on my own.

Thousands of people came to the Barton Coliseum to see us march across the stage and all together throw our tassels to the other side as the class of 1979 graduated from Little Rock Central High School. The future appears to be bright.

CHAPTER 17

Into The Future

In 1978, the Supreme Court ruled in Regents of the University Of California V. Bakke that special admissions programs, which are designed to assure the admissions of a specified number of students from certain minority groups, were unlawful. Thus stating that these programs designed to diversify higher-level education were reverse-racism and therefore unconstitutional.

The Bakke decision was in favor of a young man who felt he had been turned down at medical schools because of quota policy for minority recruitments helped us realize that things were about to change again, and not in our favor. The decision guided the country to gradually take away laws and policies designed to level the playing field purposively for people who had been discriminated against for centuries. Venerable black universities like Howard Medical School, which had been established in answer to oppression and blatant segregation, were now mandated to allow whites to compete in their admissions process.

It is a new decade and the Yuppies *(Young Urban Professional), the Hippies of the sixties and early seventies, are running the corporate world.*

Ronald Reagan is the U.S. president and his economic policy known as Reaganomics was set up to make the wealthy richer. The benefit of this plan was supposedly to trickle down and help the less fortunate. Most of the poor never felt the trickle because it never came.

Cocaine became the drug of choice and drug cartels in Central and South America shipped drugs into the U.S., which changed the social fabric of the inner city. Street dealers became younger with the introduction of crack, a derivative of cocaine that is smoked. For many inner-city youths, education became secondary to the fast money that drug dealing brought to the scene. Not only were drugs flowing rapidly, another problem came with it; the arrival of West Coast gangs started to emerge locally causing increased crime and bloodshed in our streets.

I spent most of the eighties attempting to find my niche in life. I enrolled in the University of Arkansas at Fayetteville to further my education and to try out for the football squad. I had been working out each summer with Big Jim, a person from my neighborhood who was an All-State football player at Central in 1974. He went to the University of Arkansas on an athletic scholarship and became an All-Conference defensive tackle. I felt with his tutelage and my grades, I would be ready for the big-time.

I wasn't able to enroll in college until the start of the 2nd semester. During my first trip to the university, I came to the realization that the stories you hear about some of the people in the northwest hills of Arkansas were not a myth. The road trip to Fayetteville seems to be broken into two stages; the pleasant part was Interstate 40 from Little Rock to Alma, and the hazardous part was Highway 71, which was a winding road through the Boston Mountain of Northwest Arkansas leading from Alma to Fayetteville. My brother, Veo and I stopped at a little mom and pop café in the mountain and immediately received a strange vibe that we were not welcome there. As soon as the door closed behind us, the entire room suddenly became quiet and the music on the jukebox was shut down. Everyone stared directly at us as if we came in there looking for trouble. In hindsight, I would not have spent a dime there now, but we embarrassingly bought a can of coke and a bag of chips and left "with the quickness".

I enrolled in all my classes and was ready to give it my best shot at higher learning. I had taken several of the "run of the mill" freshmen level classes like Freshman Composition, Political Science and Sociology. I also took a Physical Education class because I was definitely going to try out for the University of Arkansas Razorbacks football team as a non-scholarship walk-on.

The Razorbacks was the only NCAA division one football team in the state and the entire state of Arkansas followed them. In a state with no other major sports team- college or professional, cheering for the Razorbacks ranks very high on the list of an Arkansan's favorite leisure activity. For many it ranks right behind fishing and hunting. At the games, you would here the chants of "Woo Pig Sooie" all throughout the event, which is an old farm call to the hog's feeding pen. The university did not have a black athlete on scholarship until 1969. This was not unusual in the south where racism flourished. However, since 1969, the Black athlete had played an important role in Arkansas' proud tradition. Race relations had changed for the better at the University just as they did throughout the south during the seventies. From what I saw and felt, however, this change seemed to have had more to do with finances than it had to do with the University being humanitarians.

It was obvious to everyone that the university needed to allow black athletes to play in order to help them win- bottom line.

One of the first things I noticed about this college is that the faculty and staff are not very personable. All I was to them was my social security number. The first class I attended was a Political Science class that had over 200 students in it. Now with a class of that size I thought how you could be somebody other than a number to the teacher. For the first time in my life, I felt like I did not have the support of my community behind me. There were 16,000 students on campus but only about 700 are African Americans. One morning on my way to class, I looked in every direction trying to make eye contact, looking for a potential friend. Hundreds of students were milling around and not one person, with the exception of me, was Black. There wasn't much of a social life for Black people in Fayetteville either. If one of the Black fraternities or sororities didn't have a dance or activity, there was simply nothing to do. The deck here seemed to be stacked against you here if you were black. Racism could rear its ugly head at any time if you did not stand up for yourself.

My goals at the University of Arkansas are similar to the goals I first had at Central High. I was going to set the campus abuzz by being a star on the football field. Big Jim had already warned me that being a star for the Razorbacks wasn't as easy as it had been at Central. First of all, you had to be swift and play on a very high level because college football was a much faster game than high school. I wasn't really worried about the swiftness because I ran a 4.4 sec. forty-yard dash in 1979 when 4.6 sec. was considered very fast. Jim also told me that being a black athlete at the University of Arkansas meant that I had to be willing to perform twice as hard as a white athlete did in order to get any recognition. He said, "Floyd you have to remember that this is a traditionally white university and when I say white, I mean lily-white. It's located in a part of the state where very few black people ever lived. I actually think it was built up in the mountain to persuade blacks not to ever want to attend school there." He explained to me that even though the social climate was changing for the better at the U of A, racism was still lurking among the staff and "these people wouldn't need much of an excuse to send you home."

Jim had seen several incidents of unfairness during his four years at the university. He was an All-American at his position and had been better than a white teammate who played alongside him. His white teammate was also named to the All-American team. The white teammate received considerably more attention and newspaper press than Jim did. In spite of the fact that Jim had numbers to prove that he was better than this teammate was on the field of play, this person was drafted in the first round of the NFL draft where he could make a whole lot more money. Jim had to settle for playing in the Canadian Football League.

Throughout the decade of the seventies and eighties, this scenario seemed to repeat itself many times. The white athlete's abilities are more important to this team and they seem to deserve more recognition for doing less. It seems that the black athlete's abilities are more so ignored, while their standards are higher.

The University of Arkansas had the facilities to provide one of the finest educations in this region of the country, but it was not eager to provide a fair education to African American students. This is a prime example of some people in southern regions of our country not wanting to give up this traditionally bigoted ways so they would not have to compete with black people. From my past experiences with the white boy in the slap boxing contest up until now, I started thinking that maybe what I heard had been right. Quite possibly, the people from Africa or the hard work during the era of slavery had made us stronger than whites as a people.

Despite these negatives working against me, I was determined to make it here. Jim had told the coaches about me and I was given the go-ahead from them to make the try-out for the team. One of the best coaches in the nation coached the Razorbacks. He was a short, charismatic, quick-witted man named Lou Holtz. Coach Holtz took over the program from the legendary coach Frank Broyles who had decided to become a full-time athletic director after the 1976 season. Holtz took over in 1977 and immediately became an instant success. He was known for putting the best athletes on the field even if he had to play them at a different position than the original one they had previously played before. He was a winner- one of the best play-callers in the history of the game.

I was going to try out for the spot of a local player from the northwest Arkansas Area. He was a defensive back who had walked onto the team the year before and earned a scholarship. I felt in my heart that I was a better football player than he was, but one of the coaches told me that this position was secure and I had better look for some other position to play. That was typical University of Arkansas Fayetteville mentality. Here is a coach telling me where I cannot play before he even saw how good a player I was; telling me where I could not play before he ever told me where I could. The truth of the matter was that this player's father was an area high school coach and a graduate of the university. Yes, I was a victim of the "good ole boy" system before I even put on pads. This was demoralizing for me. But it happens, and I was not going to let it hold me down. I was determined to make star player on the University of Arkansas team. However, another roadblock was insurmountable. I could not resolve a class scheduling conflict between the team and my academic requirements. The coaches wanted all of the walk-on players to take special classes where we were to study the playbook and defensive schemes, but I couldn't be there at the proper time. Not knowing previously about any special playbook classes, I had already enrolled in a freshmen composition mandatory English class that I couldn't reschedule to another time.

When I would show up for practice, one coach in particular always asked me why I had not attended the play class. No matter how many times I explained to him the conflict, he would ask me the same question again and again. He never offered any solution to the problem and held the fact that I couldn't make the class against me. At that time, I thought that maybe this coach had forgotten what I told him about the class scheduling conflict. In hindsight, I know in order to be a good coach; it requires you to have a photographic memory.

It appeared that the cards were stacked against me as far as being a football star at the U of A, but I persisted and started gaining the favor of many coaches. The inter-squad Red-White games were approaching and we were scheduled to play two live action games; one in Fayetteville and another one a week afterwards in Little Rock. These games helped the coaches evaluate our progress in picking up our assignments on defense. Before these games, I decided I would do some individual workouts on my own. I went to the track field and ran a few hurdles. One day, from out of the corner of my eye, I spotted a well- endowed, nice looking female running in a bikini- no less, on the other side of the track! I'm a young guy and I had never seen anything like this where I came from. Needless to say, my concentration got broken. I embarrassed myself by tripping over a hurdle and injuring my knee. I would have received the necessary medical attention to correct this injury if I had been a scholarship player. But since I was a mere walk-on, I don't feel the university thought it was worth it. Finally, I left pro football star dreams and getting a college education at the University of Arkansas Fayetteville alone.

CHAPTER 18

Working Man

After my ill-fated attempt at college football, I decided to return home to Little Rock and become a working man. My brother Andrew was a keyboard player for one of the more successful bands in the Little Rock area, called Soul Mind & Body (SMB). SMB played top forty rhythm and blues music. They played many clubs and proms in the area. Andrew and the guys allowed me to be their sound and lighting man wherever they performed.

I also decided to give back to my community what I had learned just as Jim had done for me. I became a little league baseball coach at Dennison Park, which was the traditionally black community park where we participated in organized sport when we weren't allow to play at the "white" ball fields.

The world was changing at a drastic rate. Crack cocaine usage has spread across the country. Teenager represented a large percentage of the pushers in the inner-city. Along with the drug came violence and gangs. The prisons became overcrowded dues to strict laws that were drafted to stop this epidemic. The money that the drugs bought to the community changed young people priorities and education was no long important to some of our people.

A fairly new genre of music was dominating the airwaves; rap music or hip-hop is a form of music that derived from spoken-word poets but was mixed in with hip music with a funky beat. Things are very different from a decade before and the biggest question is how we are going to corral this problem.

During the school year of 1987 second semester, Mr. Everett Hawks, the principal of Central High School, hired two extra campus supervisors. Jerry Smith and Floyd Smith were hired to help out Benny Johnson and Jackie Fells. When we met with Mr. Hawks in his office, he explained how he wanted us to work our jobs and who would be our supervisor. He also explained to us that many of the teachers there were really good. For the majority of the teachers, we already knew this to be true from when we were students here ourselves. He said that he wanted us to get very familiar with all of the students here and to be friendly with them. We must be there for the student's needs and at the same time make sure they do what they are supposed to do. I think the tallest order and potentially most hazardous one at that time was that we had to keep people who didn't belong there away from the campus. That was pretty much how our meeting went with Principal Hawks. He detailed how and what we were supposed to be doing for the students and teachers on the campus during the day. After the meeting, he asked us to go out and re-introduce ourselves to the teachers who already knew us, and to let them know we would now be working here as campus supervisors. He asked us to chat with the teachers and make a favorable impression with the ones who did not know us.

After we met with most of the teachers, we went back to the office and got together with all of the administrators and vice principals. We received our work details and where we would be stationed at the beginning of the school day, during lunch and after school let out. We were instructed as to what would be our responsibilities and duties in the classrooms. Our supervisor's name was Ms. Ellen Linton. She gave each individual campus supervisor a job specification and their work detail.

My work detail during the morning hours was on 16th Street. This is how I got a chance to see how all of the people who didn't go to school would hang out there in front of QT's.

QT's was a video game room on the corner of 16th and Park Streets, directly across the street from Central High School. If there ever was a business in the wrong place, this was it. This business was a classic temptation to students who weren't interested in getting a good education and it was a distraction to those who were. It also served as a hangout for non-students who just wanted to hang around the school and socialize with our students. In addition, coming from QT's, we had a bunch of people who would just drive by the school. At least fifty or more would regularly get in their cars and just parade around the school. Some days there would be so many people hanging out on the side of QT's; it was like a big picnic to them. That was one of our main problems in the morning hours. People that didn't go to school there would come by and hang out.

About twenty or more buses would pull up every morning and drop off students. The kids would file off the buses and up onto the campus. Some of them would mill off to the back and some would hang out in the front of the campus and do what young kids do; laugh and talk, review their homework, discuss the latest fad, etc.-about the same thing we used to do. A lot of students would stand around out in the front of the building every morning waiting for the bell to ring.

At that time, we still had an awful lot of students who would smoke cigarettes. We didn't have a no-smoking policy then, so students would smoke right there on campus. After all the buses arrived and all the students got on campus, they would finally go to their classrooms and the tardy bell would ring. It was then our responsibility to go inside the hallways and run the late ones to class.

Almost every day, it would be at least fifteen minutes after the tardy bell rang that we would still be running students to their classrooms. We would have to rush them out of the bathrooms, out the hallways and nooks and crannies, run them from outside of the doorway and into their classrooms. Eventually, we would get all of them in class. They would be in class about 45 minutes or so and we would have about a 45 minutes break. Then the bell would ring for them to change class and it would start all over again, but not as bad as it was in the morning.

Another one of our problems, which I thought was pretty bad, was that we had kids smoking who would go out around the doorway, hang outside, and smoke their cigarettes. And there wasn't anything we could do about it until after the five minute bell rang. After that bell would ring, then we could go and force them- non-physically, to put out their cigarettes and go to their classrooms. And again, like I said, it would be 10 to 15 minutes after the tardy bell rang that we would still be running after kids to get them to their class.

We had two lunches. During the third period, the students who had 3rd period classes on the north side would have the first lunch period. The ones that had 3rd period on the south side would eat lunch the second session. Therefore, we would have half the school eating lunch while the other half would be in school. We had to separate the lunch crowd away from the kids that would have to remain in class.

We attempted to keep it relatively quiet and would pull gates around the section of students who were having lunch in order to keep them from going on the side that was still in class. I was stationed in front of one of the gates and Benny would be stationed at the other one. We had other security as well; one of them probably would be down at the cafeteria and the other one would be outside of the cafeteria keeping an eye on the student's movements.

Our policy was an open campus. Kids could leave campus and go get lunch at that time. Those who had cars drove or would jump in cars with their friends and drive away to home, McDonald, Burger King or something like that and get their lunch. Also, there were always those we didn't know where they had been because some of them would come back under the influence of alcohol or whatever. We could tell by teenager's silliness of their behavior, lack of control, or by how hyperactive they would be.

This was my first year of a learning experience. This was the first time I had ever worked on a campus and gotten around to see so much of what was really going on as a campus supervisor. I was learning from Benny and Jackie. We were all learning from the vice principal and the principal also, so we kept getting better at our job and it became more and more interesting as we went along.

We would often have non-students come onto the campus, so we had to really watch out for that. Eventually we found out who was and was not supposed to be there, and would turn them away. Nevertheless, for some reason, they would always come back. We had suspected that drugs were on campus from the beginning.

The tardy bell would ring and for 10 or fifteen minutes afterwards, until lunch period was over for everybody, we would still be running students to their classes. Eventually we would get them into classrooms. Most of the kids would go on to class and some of them skipped anyway. Those that were skipping, we turned in to their vice-principal.

When it came to the end of the school day the first year that I started working at Central, the procedure was that after the bell rang for everybody to get out of school, we would first help load up the buses that went south. The east bus parked in front of the school. The buses that went west and north parked on 16th Street. Many of the students who drove to school would park in the parking lot on 14th Street. Some of the drivers would park around on the sides of the campus. While school was being let out, we still had a problem with a bunch of young men who didn't go to school there. They would get in their cars and drive around our school. A lot of them would come and hang out on the wall at QT's across the street. This was a continuing problem we had to deal with. We had to deal with all the problems in the neighborhood approaching our students. About 10 or 15 minutes after the bell rang, we would finally let the bus go and push everybody on home.

CHAPTER 19

What's Going On? 1987-88

Invariably, it would begin at the end of the week, usually on a Friday when the students would go out. A lot of them would go out and somehow get admitted into nightclubs. Then a problem would often develop at the nightclub somewhere over the weekend. When we returned to school on Monday, we would often have these cliques of girls that had a problem with some other girls. That is when serious trouble would commence. Occasionally it would be a guy who had a problem with another one, but mostly, the main problem would usually be over a guy. Somebody went out with somebody's boyfriend. Or somebody's friend saw her with who she thought was her boyfriend with this other girl who went to school there, etc..

When we'd return to school after the weekend, these wild girls would be so keyed up, that we'd walk into an all out fight in progress. Girls would be fighting as soon as we got to school that next morning. Early on a Monday morning, they would be fighting?! We would see them congregating in the hallway, and we would have to run and get our radios. Then we would have to fight our way through a crowd of 100 or so people to break the crowd up in order to make it to these girls. Some of the students would be routing for their favorite. Then we had to separate them without getting scratched or injured ourselves. A lot of times, we pulled the ones that were fighting into one of the nearest classrooms just to get them away from the crowd that had gathered. The other security guard would transfer the opposing group of girls upstairs. Then we would clear out the hallways so we could get all the girls who were involved up into the vice principals office. We'd finally get them all up into the vice principals office and from that point on, the vice principal would take over and deal with them.

Things would go smooth again for about a few days, then these same girls would often start it back during lunch time. One particular day during lunch, a fight broke out while we were in the parking lot. We ran right away from our lunch duty assignments to get some of the other security guards to help break these girls up. It often took more than one of us to break these girls up because some of them really meant to do each other in. Some of them brought home made weapons; cut off baseball bats and spikes, brass knuckles, bicycle parts, a piece of steel they had picked up and brought to school with them in their purse- you name it. For whatever reasons, it was an ongoing fight this year with breaking up girls from fighting.

Anyway, we made it to close to the end of the 1987-88 school term. Traditionally, all of the seniors would skip class at the end of the term and go to the park. They would have a water gun fight. They called it a "Wet Fest" in which all of the seniors participated. Suddenly, one day we looked around and most of the students weren't there. It was kind of spooky, you know. Later on, we discovered that all of the seniors were at the park with water guns, wetting everybody down. When they got tired of that, they got buckets of water and poured it on folks! That was our first year experiencing this, but now we are warned about what happens on senior SKIP day from now on.

Senior skip day has passed a few days ago and now it is time for the semester's final exams. The seniors would have taken their exams 2 weeks earlier before everyone else. After the juniors took their final semester exams, they met somewhere and organized a caravan. The juniors put on all black and gold and they painted themselves up in black and gold. It was about 50 or more cars involved decorated in black and gold. They took the senior class flag and circled the school waving the flag and whooping it up in the caravan. Then they hit up Hall High school. They threw water balloons and eggs around that school. When they left Hall High, they went over to Parkview and caravanned around there and did the same thing. Then after they left those two rival schools, they went over to Mount St. Mary or another High School somewhere else in the district. Then they finally made their way on back to Central. They circled the entire school three times, blowing their horns. Usually, the kids didn't throw eggs at their own school, but some of them threw water or squirted water balloons on whoever was out there while they circled the block. When they finished circling the block about the third time, they pulled up into the *senior* parking lot, parked their cars and ran, jumped or danced their way back up to the school. By the time they returned to school, we pretended to be all upset with them and ran them on to class. At that time, that is just how we dealt with caravanning at the end of the year.

So, we made it through the year and we got down to graduation time at the Barton Coliseum. Central's graduation was still being held there and we would still pack the house. There would be at least ten thousand people there on graduation night. After the graduation ceremony, the seniors had the Project Graduation. Everyone would meet at War Memorial Park and leave their cars in the parking lot there, then ride the bus to a place they called at that time, SOB or Shrimp Oyster and Beerhaus located in the East End of the city. They would stay there from approximately 10p.m. until about 5a.m. the next morning, partying, dancing, shooting pools and playing cards. We campus supervisors stayed there with them until the end, providing security for them. This would be our last activity with these seniors and we'd say our goodbyes and give them all our best wishes at this time.

We would be sleepy and tired, but we had to return to school the next morning and finish off the rest of that day adhering to our regular duties. We finally made it to the end of the school year and began the rest of the younger student's semester exams. It takes three days to do all the rest of the final semester exams. On the last day, after they've finished their exams and after the last school bell rang for that year, all the kids opened up their lockers. They took their books and started throwing books and papers down the hall. They started screaming. They started hollering like crazy. They were glad. They took so many books and papers and threw them down the hallways, there would be tons of it, tons of stuff; water balloons, eggs- Everything! This was the first year I had worked there during the final semester and I was amazed that this was going on. I didn't know what I should be doing about it, but I took the lead from the older supervisors and just got out of their way.

We went outside and tried to control some things out there, but mostly we made sure the buses are ready to take them HOME. The students are outside and happy and still throwing books, paper, throwing water balloons, shooting water etc.; but we put them on those buses. We sent the buses on their way and waited with the rest of the kids who were waiting on a ride from their parents until they came. I was happier than they were when it was the finish of the last day of the school year. It was pretty much a rough year for me. It was my first year being a campus supervisor and it was truly a learning experience.

Thereafter, what Ben, Jackie, Jerry and I decided is that we would learn from that last year's experience. For the next year, we're going to work out, we're going to run and come back in better physical condition. We're going to be better campus supervisors. We're going to be more like super campus supervisors that next year. That was our goal. We worked out all that summer like we used to do when we were athletes ourselves, getting ready for the next year; the 1988-89 school year.

CHAPTER 20

All in a day's work

During the summer of 1988, Benny, Jackie Jerry and myself Floyd exercised a lot during the summer getting ready for the 88/89 school year. Benny had a weight room up at the Carver room at the YMCA on 14th Street. A lot of times, we would go there or to the Dunbar Recreation center and lift weights. In addition, we did a lot of running. We might have run about 3 miles a day, five days a week. We thought that by exercising, running and lifting weights we would be prepared for the upcoming school year of 88/89. From our past experiences, we'd had a lot of heavy physical activity to do: carrying people on stretchers, lifting and resetting barriers, and a lot of running. Always we had to run to the places where serious activity was going on. And there were various other situations that occurred that we might have to help out with. So, we worked out all summer long. Finally, summer ended for us around the last half of August and it was time to start back to school.

We were notified to come to Central and meet with the principal and get our work detail right before school started. School had an orientation, so we got a chance to meet some of the new tenth graders who were coming in in order to get to know them before school starts the new season. Since it was our second year, we got more familiar with many of the 11th and 12th graders too. It is important for us to get to know the students individually. That way we'll know how to help them out, and if necessary, be better able to secure the school. After the orientation, we went back to Mr. Hawk's office. This year, he issued some gold caps and gold shirts for us to wear every day. When we arrived on the first day of school, we had on our gold supervisor shirts and caps; Very nice. We started walking around the campus like this and greeted the teachers again. When we greeted them and introduced or re-introduced ourselves, they told us how happy they were that we had returned to Central and what a great job we had done the previous year. This made us feel good and motivated us to do an even better job this year.

We got our work detail from Principal Hawks. Where he wanted to place us individually to work would be posted at a certain time of the day now. From the first day of school this year, we had our own separate post. Most of our students returned to school the first week of the school year. The first week went real well with no incidents whatsoever.

Now we're down to when football Season starts. It is our duty to work the ball games. At that time, we weren't searching anyone. The school district did not have an official searching policy or procedure. All we were hired to do was to watch everyone who came in, report anything looking suspicious, and make sure nothing bad broke out during the games. The first game was normal. It went pretty well. Everyone is happy to be back in school and we're watching the game closely because we had a good team that year.

One of the guys who used to play with the team could not play anymore because he had injured himself during one of the football games. The football players usually get out about five minutes before the end of class. The injured player's classes would end and they would push his wheelchair where he had to go and carry him up the steps to his next classes. This was the only way he could continue to attend school at Central was by his football teammates doing this for him. He was a real good guy. We all liked him very much, so we are also glad to see him back to school.

We had the first pep assembly before the first football game during which the coach introduced all of the starters and players to the student body. Well, this school year, they felt it was necessary to have extra security. Another person would be working campus supervisor with us; Jerome Simms was a real good worker. He had experience working around for the entire school district. His first appointment he started working at a High School was Parkview, right before we started working at Central. Then he had been assigned to Forest Heights before he was re-assigned to help us out at Central. In addition we were all previously acquainted from when we played varsity in high school. Jerome had played football for Parkview. Benny had played for Hall, and I played for Central along with Jackie and Jerry. All of us had been former football stars in the district. We were lucky to have him at this time with his experience. It worked out excellent for us all the way around, and just in time.

It was only the second week of school when it started all over again. It was the girls coming in complaining about other girls messing with their boyfriend. We started having deadly fights again. We were breaking up fights left and right between the same girls and having to take them to the vice principal's office. Through the vice principal, we found out that a lot of the fights were over one particular boy and they were serious about it. Then we would have to break up the fights and the vice-principal would have to discipline the girls. It kind of made me want to find that particular guy and talk to him about it.

CHAPTER 21

Environmental Issues

That year we had a different environmental problem also. At that time, in late summer, it was still hot. Some days the temperature was triple digits and the school didn't have an air conditioner. There were fans, but there weren't any air conditioners. The building was so hot this particular year that many people fainted. We would have to go get the nurse and trot up and down stairs with the stretcher to wherever. Thankfully, it would mostly be lightweight girls that fainted. We would have to carry the fainted person out of the classroom and help the nurse carry them into her station. A lot of days, this would happen more than once. I'll tell you, it would be about a half a dozen or so times a day we would have to do that during the hot spell. One young lady, we had to transport three times in one day. That was one of the serious situations we had to deal with.

During the morning hours, we would have to constantly deal with people who didn't go to Central High coming over and hanging out there. It would be called vagrancy and nothing more. A lot of people would be hanging out at QT, like I said; just hanging out all day at QT's and doing nothing. At that time, we still had open campus, so a lot of the students who walked to school would go over there and hang out. It started becoming real crowded over there now, more so than the previous year.

We began to have a lot of traffic in the morning hours; people riding by, cruising in their cars circling the block and playing their music real loud. When the bell rang, we would have to press everybody to his or her class real hard. Many times, it would take 15 to 20 minutes to get the late students to their class even after the tardy bell rang. Smokers would still be hanging around the doors on the outside of the school leading to the classroom. We always had to deal with that. So we would get all that done. When it came time for second period, we might have another problem. A fight would break out and we would have to deal with that. Quite a few smokers would run to the doors again- doors on the south in a circle, and hang out on doors on the north end. They would be grouped up, out there smoking in five to ten people. We dealt with that on a daily basis. During lunchtime, we also had problems off-campus. The students could go off campus, buy their lunch and come back. An incident might occur off campus and a lot of students would go out for lunch and not return.

CHAPTER 22

There's a New Kid in Town

There was this one particular guy that we started watching this year. He was from a school out of Texas. He had long hair; hair to his shoulders and he would wear all black, expensive motorcycle boots and always wore sunshades. We had to watch him because we knew he was dealing dope inside the school. We would kick back and watch him carefully. We were trying to catch him in the act. We watched him closely for a couple of weeks deciding how to turn him in with the evidence. We saw several students go up to him and he would give them a matchbox to light a cigarette with or something. Now that wasn't against the rules to have matches to light cigarettes with, but we still couldn't figure out what and how was he passing dope. Was he passing something to them or was he just giving them a matchbox to light something with. He was smart, so we never did see any money transaction between him and the students. But we put pressure on him and kept our eye on him like flies. He only lasted a couple of months in school, after he was on to us, until he eventually just dropped out. I checked his record and found out that he had been 21 years old that year, anyway. That was probably only one of the reasons he didn't stay for the next semester.

During the '88 – '89 year at the end of the term, we still had a problem at school. About 21 or 22 buses would pull up every day. The buses that kids took would go east and south on Park Street. The buses that would go north would park on 16th Street. At the end of the day, we would be posted by name at various locations around the school. One of my posts was on 16th street at the end of the day. At that time we did not block that street off. At least one hundred or more people would drive around the school. These would be guys. A lot of them had been hanging out across the street on the wall at QTs. Sometimes fights would break out between one of our students and a guy across the street. That year we had many fights at the school. So we would send the buses on and go and call all the security to the place where the fight was going on and break it up.

Still, however, this year the majority of our fights would be between girls. And I mean they would be scrapping. A crowd would circle around the fight and we would literally have to fight our way through the crowd. It could be as large as a hundred kids, so we had to dive right through and physically force our way in there to break up the fight. Really, we had to fight the crowd of on-lookers before we could get to the fight.

Then one day after school, after everybody got out of school and we got off work, we saw something peculiar. Young men were frog walking with books on their head. We would drive by Central and we noticed there would be crowds of boys with books on top of their head. There was another group on the football field doing the same thing. _So_ what was this? We started investigating. Why are these students coming up here to our campus doing this? A lot of them were in the missionaries and at the time, they would call them fraternities.

What they called a fraternity, we called gang. These antics were how they used to initiate new gang members. All these kids would return to campus after everybody left or they would wait around until after 5 o'clock. This went on for a while. We informed the principals and vice principals what these kids were doing and what was going on in the neighborhood. At that time, we didn't have any gang fights, so it wasn't considered a big issue. Although it was after school hours, we still kept watch because we knew what was brewing. We kept an eye on each one of them when we noticed how they started dressing differently at school. They started wearing T-shirts and colored T-shirts replaced regular button up shirts. The groups kept getting bigger and bigger. Then the other groups would perform when they'd see these groups of guys and what they were doing, and vice versa. We didn't know the meaning of how they were acting out at that time, but we learned the interpretation of gang displays. Someone else would create a group also and they'd call it a fraternity, or gentleman's club, brotherhood and so on. So, it was on the rise. We saw it coming.

After watching the behavior of a few guys that came from Texas, we started asking the students around where they were from. We got to hearing about a lot of students who came from California. Some of them were girls, but most of them were guys. And then, most of these new students had come from Chicago. They had moved from Chicago, Dallas, Los Angeles and the big urban areas into Little Rock so they could go to school in peace. This is what they told me; how bad it was in California and the other mentioned places. Many of the kids and a lot of their friends and family members were getting killed by gang violence. Their parents had moved them back here with a family member where things were quieter. It was the same way in Chicago. A lot of kids talked about how a lot of their friends had gotten killed then in Chicago. From the stories they told, Chicago had terrible gangs. Then again, their people had sent them down here to go to school in Little Rock where many of them ended up at Central High. So we were getting a lot of students from all over the country coming to school at Central. Their families had sent them to Little Rock to go to school and some of them were starting their own *fraternities* here.

For the past several months or so there were a lot of cliquey girls having fights. These sets of girls we broke up in the fights had homemade weapons. One of them had welding iron rods she had taken considerable time to group and tape together. Another had barbed wire hooked up onto hers. You might have another girl we'd have to take some things out of her purse. You'd have another girl with a small baseball bat splintered so that it would cut. Another would have a nail or something sticking out of the end of her small club. And we would have girls that would carry plain old knives and box cutters. One of the girls we saw fighting pulled out a knife. Jerome saw it and tried to get to the girl so he could take the knife from her, but she and a group of girls ran into the girl's restroom. When they ran in there for cover, Jerome called all security to his aid. He had had to block and hold the door by putting his arm and his foot against it. He had them all blocked inside the bathroom while about seven or eight young girls were pushing against it trying to escape. Jerome managed to block the door and kept them from getting out until we got there. The vice principal had always told us that when we're faced with a situation like that, to holler in there to the girls and let them know that we're coming in and then go. Let them know that males are coming in the girl's restroom, and then go in. When we rushed over there in answer to Jerome's call, all us of gave them a warning. We went on in there and checked some girl's purses. Then one of the female vice principals ran in there while we were doing that.

We searched the bathroom all over and found out that the girl who had the knife had ditched it somewhere. One of the windows was cracked a little bit and we knew immediately what had happened. We found out that they had handed the knife to someone outside the window and we never did find it. But even though we never saw the knife again, they had enough to discipline the girls and send them home because they had been going at it for days. We let all of the other young ladies out of the bathroom. All, except the one particular girl who had the knife; and with the exception of this one girl who refused to come out because she was very shy. We had to search them and she didn't want to leave the restroom until all the people in the hallway had cleared out because she was embarrassed. We were embarrassed that we had to invade their privacy like that too, but there was no alternative. We cleared the hallway out and sent everyone else who was just hanging around to see what was going on back to class. She finally came out visibly shaken and we let the vice-principal handle the situation from that point on.

By now, we are familiar with the majority of the students here. We still had problems with people that didn't go to school here. They would walk up on campus and want to walk through the school or the cafeteria. We would spot them and go up to them and ask if they are students here at Central. Most of the time, a lot of them would say yes they are. So we would question them. And they would tell us, "Yeah, I'm just a new student, uh uh, I just started today, uh, I'm been going here you just haven't seen me, um...you see me all the time", etc.   I would then say, "O.K. what grade are you in?" They would tell me what grade they were in. If they would say, I'm in the 10th grade. We would say O.K., then... We would ask for example: "What or who is the tenth grade vice principal?" If they couldn't answer that, we would ask them another question: "Who is your English teacher?" By this time we know all the tenth grade English teachers, all the tenth grade math teachers and for the 11th and 12th grades, we would know all the teachers by this time. If they couldn't answer who is your English teacher, we would ask, "Who is your math teacher?" Most of the time, they couldn't answer. Finally they would say, "O.K. I'm going to tell you the truth. I'm just coming around here looking to see how things are here." Well, you can't just come around Central High just to look around like that. So we would have to ask them to leave. That was an ongoing problem. I don't know if the visitors were trying to distribute drugs, find their girlfriend or whatnot, or even leave a bomb. They may have been sightseeing just like they said, but that problem went on all year. It was the same with the fights. We were beginning to have fights all year.

CHAPTER 23

School Spirit

When we would have a pep assembly inside the auditorium for the football or the basketball team, for some reason, the majority of the white students would try to leave. They used pep assemblies just as an opportunity to skip school. We also had some blacks, but the majority of the people at the school who would try to leave early would be white students. We had to position ourselves all the way around the school in order to keep them from leaving. A lot of them would know in advance when we were scheduled for the pep assembly, so they would have a parent call up to the office and check them out. That was O.K., but the ones who didn't check out first with their parents would run from us. They'd run to their cars and jump in and drive around the block and pick up friends. That would happen if they got lucky and campus supervisors didn't catch them. Most of the times, we were smart enough and still fast enough to catch everybody and direct them to the auditorium for the pep assembly. After we'd get them there, we would still have to keep watching them to keep them in there.

The next time we'd see them they'd be so-o mad; "Why do we have to stay here for this ol' pep assembly anyway? I don't see no use for having a pep assembly, I don't even like the ol' nasty football game"...or some such. And we'd say "Well, we just can't let you leave because the principal tells us it's good for the school spirit and he tells us what to do. If you don't like the rules, you'll have to consult with the principal.

CHAPTER 24

The Crying Time

During this school year, 1989, one of the teachers was working at the school after hours on February 18th around 5:24p.m.when he discovered smoke in the wall on the first floor. He ran and called the fire department. The fire department came to the school and found out there was an electrical fire in the wall. The fire cost at least $75,000 worth of damage. If that teacher had not been working after hours, the school probably would have had a lot more damage than $75,000.00. With an electrical fire in the walls, Central High might have burned down to the ground. That was one significant incident that occurred during the school year of 1989. It was also a bad year in general for the school district.

There were several school shootings throughout the district. There was also a very young kid who got shot up at Henderson Jr. High School that year. There was a shooting at a school bus stop that year. We began to get worried because we knew that everything; all the major youth activity was centered on Central High. Up to that time, most of the serious problems we had to deal with had come to Central by way of personal conflicts spilling over from some other schools or venue. We had never had anyone shot or any shootings at our school up to this time. But shootings suddenly began to occur at our school also.

The grim reaper began to visit Central's district as well from the bigger cities. I surmise it came through the new fraternities and brotherhoods that we'd seen forming a few months ago. A shooting happened in our parking lot one evening. That was the first time for Central. This new violence was not from or just at Central at that time during the 1989 school year, but it had grown out all over the district. Unfortunately judging from the news media, it looked like it was here to stay. Before it was all over with, these gangland shootings would get worse, much worse, before they got better. During this year, the entire school district was having lots of problems with violent students. Essentially, we would get more than our share.

We campus supervisors also worked the football games and other athletic functions after hours. Most of the students who attended them came to have fun and all would usually be fine. Often now, more and more, we had a difficult time with some of the fans because they were coming to the games drunk or on some kind of drug. We had to stick around these fans and keep them straight during the games. That was now one of our main responsibilities during the foot ball games. We had to spend time looking out for aggressive and obnoxious behavior.

Our roughest game was called the *Bell Bowl* game. This was when Central played the Hall High Warriors. The house would always be a packed for this game. On that day we would always have a pep assembly which would be held out in front of the school. That is where we would have our pep assemblies on this *Bell Bowl* day. The entire student body would be wild. They made special preparations for Hall High, which was our number one rival. The kids painted up their faces, painted bells on their faces and wore anything and everything black and gold. Due to huge attendance, the staff moved this game to a Saturday. So that rather than playing Hall on a Friday evening, we would have to come back to the field and play them on a Saturday morning. They also considered that if these two rivals played each other in the daytime, it would not be as tough to handle the crowd as it had been in the late evening. There wasn't much difference, however, because we still got the usual crowd. Central eventually won the games in 1989, but it was very rough and the crowds were wild.

One of our students would keep jumping off the stand and running with the flag on Central's side across on to Hall's side. This made a spectacle because we'd have to chase him, catch him and put him back up in the stands. Then he might pass the flag to someone else and we would have to do the same thing over again for that one. Those games with Hall High would be wild for us. When the game was over, we'd have to go outside the football arena to the streets and make sure the fans were safe. We really worked hard during these game times. We also had a lot of people who wanted to continue to hang out and wouldn't go home. They just wanted to stand around and wait for the people to leave. Some of them wanted to see their friends, I guess, but we had no idea what some of them might be up to.

At last, the game problems had ended for this year. Later on that year, an activist we called "Say" Macintosh kept coming up there with some pigs. He was protesting how the students were leaving the parking lot. He brought a group of pigs on campus a couple of days. At least he kept them tied up. Where he got the pigs, I don't know, but that was his way of protesting how the students were keeping the campus and surrounding area unclean. It would be a mess some days before we left for home.

Also during the '89 school year which unfortunately happened to be one of the worst years in the schools' history, we had a lot of foreign exchange students to enter our school. They came to Central from Holland and Russia. We had a couple from France. We had them coming from all over the world and we became friends with a couple of them. One of them was a photographer from France. One day he just started following us around and taking pictures. He wanted to lift weights and work out at the Y, so he started showing up there looking for Benny Johnson. We would meet with him and started doing some things just for fun so he could learn more about Little Rock. He always had his camera with him and took pictures wherever we'd go, but he was a real regular guy and we had good fun with him that year from Paris France. I never forgot that funny kid and he became a very good friend of ours. We said we would even go visit his family in France one day.

Everyone had had enough of that year working with no air conditioner. One of the campus supervisors had started seeking other employment. It wasn't until around November, however that they decided Central would finally get a heating and cooling unit. According to my notes, it was on Nov. 20, 1989 they finally started taking out the old radiator units and throwing them away. We helped pile them up and they brought in the engineers with maybe a half million dollar air conditioner unit inside of Central. We were overjoyed because the heat waves gave us serious problems. As I said earlier, a lot of young women and a couple of men had fainted because of the heat. That made us have to tow in with stretchers, pick them up wherever they had fallen, take them out from wherever they were-the gym, classrooms, the bathroom, and tote them into the health room. They would cool off in the air conditioned nurses station. Sometimes this would go on for several days. I remember one girl we had to go pick up three times in one day. And another one, we had to pick up for five days straight. So it was a big problem. When we got this air condition unit, it was quite a relief. It also cooled us off because we had to do a lot of running. We were required to do a lot of things in the heat- terrible heat, so it became a big relief to us.

Yeah, these things happened. When we go back and look at such a history, even though we had a lot of negative things going on, that was only like 1% of the student body that would create problems in the school. When you go back and look at the academic history in Central High and see the achievements that all of the students made over the years, it more than makes up for that 1% delinquency. A lot of times you hear about all of the disapproving things, but you don't hear about many of the good things that the students themselves achieved. We are writing this book so that people will know the truth about what went on at our school; both the bad and the good. If they read this book and never went to Central, I would ask that people visit Central High, go to a year book and read about our many Hall of Fame students and what they did and have done since. See what extraordinary types and kinds of persons this school did produce.

Nevertheless, like I say, this was the year 1988-89. I believed the violence would get worse before it got better, unfortunately. And believe me, it did. I can remember that during this 1989 year, I wrote up a student for cursing loud down the hallway. The principal sent him home and told him to bring his Mother back for consultation. His mother came and confronted me in the hallway. She told me her son said that I was always harassing him, which was far from the truth. If anything it was the other way around. I patiently explained to her that no, I never harassed her son. I don't harass any of the students. It was only that he was cursing down the hallway and it is my job to write up any student who uses foul language or acts disrespectfully in school. Later on that year, this same young man was walking to school and some *fraternity* guys passed by him in a car and shot him in his back. He died later on that year. Like I said, the painful reality was this situation of killing kids was steadily getting worse right before our eyes. It got a lot worse before it got any better. This is when serious gang problems really started happening around Central High School. We were seeing all this and it was heartbreaking. We campus supervisors, Jerry, Benny, Jackie and I were trying to do what we could then to stop it.

CHAPTER 25

Stop the Violence

"On October 11, 1989, right after the homecoming parade we were having a pep rally on a mild morning. I, Big Ben Johnson, was in the courtyard when I spotted five non-students approaching the campus. I called Mr. Peterson."

"I'm Floyd Smith: During homecoming parade, I was working the south end and I told him that 5 students were walking his way. Mr. Peterson got back with me and told me that he knew the kids; that they attended Hall High."

"I'm Jackie Fells: I made a statement to Mr. Peterson if he was sure that it was OK for those kids to be here? Mrs. Faison the Vice-Principle and I walked across the street to watch a crowd of kids and we noticed a Red Devil mascot hanging in the tree- a mannequin of some sort.

We walked around and told the kids to take it down. Then we walked on back down the street to the next problem. When we glanced back around, the Red Devil was on fire! Mrs. Faison ran back to the article that was on fire. She took a stick and knocked it down trying to put out the fire, but it fell onto the car. Then the car caught on fire. I guess it started burning the paint on the corner of the car. The guys that Mr. Peterson said were OK to be on campus looked at the car and said "Those white boys have set that guys car on fire!" Even though it was an accident, some of the girls passed the word around that some white kids had started a big argument about the car. They went looking for their friend who owned the car and told him the white folks had set his car on fire, etc. That is when sporadic fights started breaking out. Before long, "All hell broke out". Blacks were attacking whites and they were trying to protect themselves and we were trying to protect everyone, but it got out of hand quickly. I would say about three hundred or so kids were fighting out in the front of the school.

That is when Jackie Fells climbed on a wall on the house across the street in front of the school. He yelled to the kids and asked them what was wrong with them. They continued to fight. That is when we had to move in hard and tough. We broke up this fight and then that fight, going from fight to fight, breaking up at least a dozen different fights. A couple of boys even tried to attack Mr. Hawks, the Principal. And one of them started to stomp on him! If it hadn't been for campus security's intervention he would have been critically injured.

I heard over the radio that one of the cars had caught on fire across the street. I ran into the building and got the fire extinguisher. As I was running out, one of the students said he could take one fire extinguisher and run across the street so Jackie could put the fire out. About that time I came out the school on the south end and that is when I spotted Security Benny Johnson running toward a group of kids holding down a white student, beating him down. They were so angry; we had to start punching the kids to get them off of him. Having just come out the school from the south end, I had no idea what was wrong with them, so I just ran behind Benny and started doing the same thing he was doing. We had to do that several times. As we were breaking up one fight, then another one would start. We worked ourselves back to Mr. Hawks where he was breaking up another fight.

Then the mood turned deadly. A crowd of angry black kids were slowly closing in on him. The rest of security jumped into the middle of that group. A lot of the black students were kicking at him now. We had to start slamming kids off of him and back toward the crowd. It was terrible. We did that several times until we got those kids off of Everett Hawks. About that time, the kids turned back around looking at us and backed away from Mr. Hawks. After we rescued Mr. Hawks, I went back into the building to my floor to get the students settled down and make sure that they were back in their classrooms on the third floor. That's when I spotted Mr. Peterson walking down the hall with a big steel pipe in his hand. I asked Mr. Peterson what he was doing with the pipe. Pete told me it was his "peacemaker". We joked about it only a few seconds before some of the teachers rushed out with their jackets and bags in hand and told me school was over for them because they were about to run and jump in their cars and go home. They told me what a good job we had done that morning though, while I was jumping back out of their way."

Jackie: "When we got things under control, we got the kids back in their classes. I observed "Pete" walking down the hallway with a pipe in his hand and I asked him what he was doing with it. He told me it was a peacemaker. I said, "What peacemaker? We are the peacemakers!" I spoke with some teachers that same day. They were getting ready to leave in a hurry until they noticed how things had quieted down. They commended us on how great a job we have been doing. That was me, Jerry Smith, Jackie Fells, Floyd Smith and Benny Johnson. Jerome was an absentee that day. When everything got under control the police came."

Benny Johnson: "Yeah about 30 minutes later they arrived- slow as usual. The Little Rock Police Department is slow! During one of our usual routine locker searches on the first floor going north, we discovered one of our students with a sketched out picture of a gang member holding a gun up to another gang member's head. The student sketched where the bullet was going through the front of the other one's head and exiting out the back. This is the student who stabbed the vice principal who turned out to be a child molester- numerous times, early one morning in her office before school started. According to an anonymous person, they heard her call him nigger, but I don't know if that was before or after the stabbing."

Floyd Smith: "After the investigation with the Campus Supervisors, Jackie Fells, Benny Johnson and myself, Floyd Smith, found out that the guy who had drawn the the sketch was the same guy that stabbed the administrator at that time."

Benny Johnson: "Willie Hutchinson, who was later identified was charged, convicted, and sentenced to the State Department of Correction here also. Carlos Patton was on his way to school one day, standing at a bus stop when a young man pulled up in a car and asked him why was he wearing the colors he was wearing? Carlos replied by saying "I can wear whatever colors I want to." When Carlos turned his back, the guy shot him in the back and killed him. A week later they had his funeral. There were many mourners- the student body. I mean he was liked really well. After that, myself; Benny Johnson, Floyd Smith, and Jackie Fells gathered at Mount Pleasant Baptist Church with the family of Carlos Patton. That is where we got the vision of the **STOP THE VIOLENCE MOVEMENT.** That is to stop the gang related crime! Also Kevin Getty was killed by a young lady over some tennis shoes that year. David Blackmon was killed by a gunshot wound that year."

CHAPTER 26

Attitude Adjustments

"After the shooting, Dr. Ruth Steel, who I feel is the best superintendent of the schools, called on Mr. Charles Springer to be the Security Czar for Central High School. It was decided that his decision regarding security would supersede everyone else. His job was to make the campus secure and safe. But he always called on Floyd, Jackie, Jerome, Benny and I to help him. A lot of times he wouldn't take our advice, but our advice had always worked. He came in with new measures where the students had to wear name tags as security badges every day. It started off on a shaky road with Mr. Springer. It was him getting to know us and us getting to know him because the teachers and everybody was made to wear those name tags."

Floyd: "There were five security people already and Mr. Springer brought in six more. He said even that wasn't enough of us to cover Central High School. He added mirrors in the halls of the school; he had a fence put around the student's parking lot to stop people from stealing cars."

Benny: "We found later that Mr. Springer wanted no longer to have us as security because we already knew our job well. He didn't think we should be friends with the students. Well, he couldn't have been any more mistaken about that. You have to be friendly to them because sometimes they are the ones that will let you know what things will occur. For example; certain fights, or if somebody would be stealing. The students are the ones that will tell us. And that was our problem with him. I definitely did not want to lose friendship with the students because they are a big happiness to our job."

"When Mr. Springer had the crew come in to put the fence around the senior lot, as the men were putting in the ten foot pole, one of the students would come by regularly and repeatedly move the pole. When the crew man came back to straighten the pole, the same student would come back and move the pole again- many times until the workers had to call Mr. Springer to the site. Mr. Springer called us campus supervisors to the site. Mr. Springer was putting on chap lip while he was talking to the man describing the student that was moving the pole: "He was wearing a red pair of shorts about 5 feet 6 inches tall..."

Floyd: "And we told him exactly who it was, "That's Aaron Burnhart."

Ben Johnson: "Mr. Springer started back putting Chapstick lip balm on his lips and said for us to go find Aaron and bring him back on site and we did. We took him to the site first, then to the Vice principle's office."

"After school, right after the buses left, I speak of a person that doesn't care about somebody's life; Mr. Springer would often tell us not to go across the street to break up a fight at QTs where a lot of activities always happen. A young man was getting beat up with a trashcan and I started to head across the street. Mr. Michael Peterson, the Vice-Principal here, summoned me to walk back toward Central, but I care about people getting seriously hurt and getting beat with trashcans. When I went on over anyhow and broke up the fight, I heard Mr.

Peterson over the walkie-talkie tell Mr. Springer to "Write Mr. Johnson up for insubordination! He didn't follow my orders not to go across the street." Well, that was O.K. with me because I have to do the right thing to live with me."

Floyd: "We told the extra supervisors to stay out of the hallway because some of the students will throw books, eggs, etc. at you especially since they don't know you. The veterans campus supervisors were outside making sure that nobody would get on the campus after Benny returned from breaking up a fight that was across the street. One of the extra campus supervisors inside called wanting backup. He needed help! Gouch was a new security officer who was trapped in the hallway while the students barraged him by throwing books at him. Jackie, Benny, Jerome, Jerry, and I heard a bunch of books hitting the walls being thrown by students on our way down the hall. We saw about fifty students with books in their hands throwing them at Gouch, the new campus supervisor. He was hovered in a corner trying to block them while books were just piled up on him and all around that corner. They saw us and the students took off running."

Benny: "I would like to take this time to say farewell to Mr. Hawks. He was the best principal in the school district. He gave us more respect than anybody, and he always told us how good we were or how good we did. Downtown at the school board were the ones that ran him away, by the way. They said they were not satisfied with his leadership and he was also deemed as insubordinate; but I think I know why. He wasn't ignorant and obstinate like some of the ones we would later get. He listened to the voices of the students and staff. He would give bonuses for Christmas and also for the summer break. So I would like to say farewell to him, a long time legend principal at Central High School, Mr. Hawks."

Jackie: "I would also say farewell to Mr. Hawks because he showed us respect and was really concerned. He also trusted us and let us handle things right around the school. I think he is the best principal also."

Jackie: "I need to add on some things about Mr. Springer. He had the big steel fence put around the students parking lot and the students felt like they were in prison. They had shirts made up with LITTLE ROCK CENTRAL HIGH CORRECTIONAL HIGH SCHOOL. Mr. Springer wanted us to get all of the T-shirts from the students because he said it was against school policy. But the students protested against it, so downtown approved for them to wear the t-shirts. This was just one of the many things going on at Central High School under Mr. Springer."

Floyd: "After the school year of **1990,** the school district decided to open up a new officer's position for everyone in the district who was interested. Several of us applied for the new position. When I read the application, it asked for a police background as one of the qualifications for an administrator. You also had to have a certificate or a college degree. Mr. Barnhouse hired someone else for that position, but he called me in to interview for another position. He asked me a lot of questions in the interview about the school. He asked me what went on at the school, how we handled certain situations and what was our daily routine. He never asked me how I felt about the job I was being hired for at all. Finally, we were told to prepare for training for our new positions that August. Mr. Barnhouse brought Montgomery and Jones in to work with us. Out of the three of them, Montgomery worked with us on hand. Montgomery asked us a lot of questions also about how to handle certain situations at the school. He also helped get the policy instituted for new security officers to get training before they were fully placed on the campus."

Benny: "I'm reporting from the transition of the campus supervisor to the director of the safety and security, Mr. (Blinky) Barnhouse. He sent out letters to the residents houses in the area to see if they wanted a job. If they did, they would have to send the return letter back in by a certain time. After doing this, they changed the name of our positions to security and safety, which is what it should have been anyway. Barnhouse, Jones, and Montgomery would ask us questions about everything that was going on and we would tell them. They would invariably say that they were not good ideas, but turn around and have to use them anyway."

Jackie: "It really surprised me how Bobby Jones came asking us every other day how we conduct things up here; how we did this, how did we do that. Then he would say that they were not good ideas. But he would use them and indicate that they were his ideas all along. I was also astonished when they didn't use one of us experienced ones to do the training instead of hiring an outside black guy and a white guy to do it. They were just feeding information off of us anyway. We worked with over 2,000 kids, knew them, and were strictly business people in getting the job done."

Floyd: "Mr. Montgomery would come to the football games and watch how we handled the crowd. He seemed especially surprised at how easily we controlled the gang members. I didn't tell him because you have to have special consideration in the community to be able to go to the head leaders and ask them to keep their guys in order."

Benny: "I also think about how Central and Hall High were a big rivalry and they had to move their games to Saturday morning because of the antagonism. They said that would help security measures. Everything was going just fine and Central had even won the game, but on the way out, this guy by the name of Poncho got shot through the windshield of a car. He ran about 2 blocks and collapsed. He was so dedicated to his gang, that when the ambulance guys picked him up bloody off the sidewalk and put him in the medical van, he started throwing up his gang signs to the other gang members!"

Floyd: "As the people were leaving, we all heard several gunshots. I yelled for all the people near me to *kneel down!!* While they were kneeling, the car that the shooter jumped out of continued rolling down 14th street. I didn't know to do anything but to run and stop the car before it did damage to something or somebody. After I stopped the car from moving, I went back up to where Benny Johnson was up ahead of me. Already he had taken the gun and had the guy that was shooting standing there also. Sometimes I remember how we did some of the things we had to do and wonder how we made it."

Benny: "We tried to get the main person who was doing the shooting. Fortunately he ran over to me and said, "Big man they shooting at me!" I immediately took the gun and told him to stand over here because nobody wanted to be getting shot at!"

Jackie: "Again, there were no police around or that incident wouldn't have happened. This should tell you how well and experienced the Central's security is and *had to be*. Once more we have shown that we knew a lot more than the new people who had been hired over us."

CHAPTER 27

EYE WITNESS

Floyd: "During this football season this year, we were charging to park cars. Our new principal was in charge of the parking lot. Every football game, we would fill up both car lots to capacity. It became so crowded he had to open up the practice football field."

Benny: "I remember the rivalry this year was between Central High and Parkview. And I mean the crowd poured in. After the game we turned in the cash for that night. It was exactly $530.00 that we turned in to Mr. H."

Jackie: "That following Monday, I and some of the security were in the campus inn eating when the bookkeeper came in. She wanted to talk to me about how many cars were parked at the game. I told her that I didn't know. I wasn't responsible for counting the cars, but it was a packed house. She replied that she knew that because she and some other coaches were there and it was indeed packed. She asked me how much money we turned in. I told her we gave Mr. H. all of it, which was $530.00. She said, "But that is not how much he turned in to me." She said he only gave her $124.00. "That is not possible, I said, because I was over-seeing the money." Then I had to stop eating and looked up at her. The bookkeeper asked me would I like to see the books on some of the other games and I told her, "Yes." I got up and walked back to the office with her to look at the books. I knew our average would be around $500.00 every football game. The record was not adding up. The latest games were all off about $200.00 to $300.00."

Floyd: "Later on that year, after we talked with safety and security, we all learned the startling fact that the money we were turning in was not matching up with what our Principal, Mr. H. turned in. After that, I told Mr. Barnhouse that I did not want to handle anymore money from that point on."

Benny: "Then it started. To get the pressure off of Mr. H., he called us into his office and said he received a call from the superintendent, Dr. Suell. He said that he had parents and students call in to say they saw the security stashing and stuffing money; to keep the pressure off of him. During that time, the administration downtown had already explained to Mr. H. that he was not to handle anymore money; no more money! He was told specifically not to handle any more. So why did he do it anyway?"

Jackie: "By the way this was after Mr. Hawks left. They called Mr. H. to oversee Central High school. This was 1990-91 school year."

Floyd: "I remember one school year- it was in the morning. I got a call over the radio that this student named Marquez was walking on the second floor with a wig on. He was causing quite a scene with a lot of other students following behind him. Mr. H. called for security to catch up with him."

Benny: "We caught up with him on the second floor and H. told us to hold him for him. So when H. got there, he said guys let's lead him out the back door, so he won't distract the other students. We went out the back door, down to the basement, and outside through the back doorway. From here we took Marquez out to 16th street and almost down to Quigley Stadium. At that time Marquez said, "Mr. H., you see these men, these real men? Now you look these men in the eyes and tell them you are not gay!" We looked at Mr. H.'s reaction, but he just stood there and didn't say anything. Then Marquez started acting very wild because Mr. H. grabbed him. He told me to grab him also. I really didn't want to, but I had to do what my boss told me to do for fear he might hit Mr. H.. So Marquez continued to struggle and said, "Mr. H. you let me go, you bitch, but Benny *you* can hold me!" Whoa!"

Floyd: "We asked Marquez why was he so mad at Mr. H.? He said because he saw Mr. H. touch another guys behind."

Benny: "Also Marquez described everything in H.'s house.(?)"

Floyd: "When Mr. H. first came to Central, he had this poster with all the fights that had taken place that year. He said we had 289 fights. The majority of the fights had been between black gang members and only one recorded as between white males. He called a a student body assembly and asked all the gang members to stand up. A large number of students stood up. He then asked us security supervisors to escort them to his office. After that we found out he had all those students who stood up suspended. I immediately knew that we were going to have even more trouble from him doing that."

Benny: "After that happened, the press came and said that's not the answer for that problem! And H. said, yes it was because he was going to have a safe and abiding school for the students and the staff. After that, he initiated locker checks and hall sweeps. The hall sweeps came about because the previous school years, there were a lot of students skipping classes. What Mr. H. would do during hall sweeps was start counting down like 5 minutes down to seconds and if the students were still in the hallways, they would have to go to detention hall."

Floyd: "During one of the football games, one of the police officers got into it and started wrestling with a gang member. After that about 30 more members of his gang stood up. Then one of the police buddies ran down the steps and we, the security, had to start tossing these guys out of the way. I mean we really had to man handle these group of guys. We got it under control and the police managed to put the original guy in handcuffs. The other gang members just walked out the stadium."

Benny: "I remember after one football game, I hadn't rested, eaten, or even been home to spend any time with my wife. Let me remind you that Floyd and I had already worked from 8a.m. to 10 p.m. That was including the previous game. Immediately after the game, Floyd and I were asked to take the cheerleaders to Clinton, Mississippi. This was really not our responsibility, but H. told us that we would get over-time for that no matter how long it was. The cheerleaders pooled their money and paid for our hotel room and meals. By the way, the cheerleaders were there for an important district competition, so it really wasn't our responsibility at all. We made it back home around midnight. The next morning of the second following day, we told H. our overtime hours and asked him when we were going to get paid. His response was, "I thought you were volunteering." He refused to pay us!

We filed a grievance against him with Frank Martin and Little Rock Teachers Association. We were scheduled to go downtown to meet with Mrs. Bernard, the Assistant Superintendent of Schools. But before we went down there, H. called me over the radio. He asked me where was my location. I told him I was over on 14th street and headed that way. He then came over to where I was and said "Mr. Johnson haven't I done a lot for you? Why are you filing a grievance against me? What is this about?" I said, "It's about a certain trip to Mississippi! I didn't get any sleep. Do you think I could just volunteer and go down there for free? Me? I am a married man and I have other responsibilities now." H. said, "So this is what this is all about- some funky money?" I said "*Duh...Yeah!*" He started to walk away and then turned his head back and said, "By the way, Mr. Johnson, I love you too." I told him "But that's not going to stop me from doing what I'm going to do." I knew he didn't have both oars in the water."

Floyd: "After we won that case, I noticed that H. would downright pick on me. He would send me to work on the third floor and then he would call me and tell me to go down to the second floor. Then he would tell me to go back up to the third floor. This kept going on and on for a while. I was talking to this older custodian and I told him about the incidents and how I thought this man was picking on me. I told him what he had me doing. He said that even if it wasn't deliberate and I was unhappy, it was time to do something about it. First, go have a talk with him. I went to Mr. H. and told him he needed to make up his mind where he wanted me to be. I said, "It looks like you are picking on me because of what we did- about the grievance and all. But by not paying people, you put yourself in that situation." The custodian was right. After that talk, I did not have any more problems with him, at least about that."

Benny: "And then during another football game where this guy had a gun. The crowd bolted and started running all over the place. While they were running, they pointed at this particular guy saying- "He's got a gun!" At this time, the guy was certainly acting disorderly. The police finally got him down and handcuffed him. They were in the process of taking him down the stairs when they became surrounded by the crip gang members. And Oh, Lord, all of us had to hold back the crowd so that they wouldn't jump on the police. They had to call for backup. Those police would have gotten hurt, believe me, if it had not been for us. I'm talking about hundreds of black kids who didn't like the police, but it took only five of us to stop them from jumping on the police. Now is that strong security? That is strong security and community respect.

I also remember when these other gang members came to a game and were trying to get in. They were some of the leaders of the crips at that time: Anthony Nash and Bobby Banks. When we refused to let them in, they cursed us out and left. After the game, we security pushed the crowd on out the way fast, as we usually do. It was on 14th or 16th Street that they started shooting at us. We had to duck and hit the ground because we could hear the bullets hitting the gates that we were standing next to. This shows you how dangerous our job was at that time."

Floyd: "That same year, the Mr. H. said he wanted to talk to us about putting on a talent show. He said he would pay us overtime cash for working security the night of this show. We knew he would not renege on us this time because of what happened last time with the Mississippi trip. So, we were all for it and told him, "Yeah." On the day of the talent show, we had everything done that we needed to do in order to get this show going. There was only one way in. We locked and chained all the other entrances. We even helped to get a huge crowd to show up. We had a table set up next to the entrance to receive the money and we searched everyone before they were allowed to go in."

Jackie: "Like Floyd said, H. came to us and we all agreed to do this talent show. We did what we needed to do to prepare for this and I observed the money being collected. One of the people collecting the money needed change, so I went to the office to get it and saw Mr. H. pouring piles and piles of money on his desk. I said to myself, "We are having a good night and that was a good fund-raiser too, but is he supposed to be handling the money?" As the talent show went on, the auditorium was packed from the bottom floor on up to the third balcony and the people were enjoying themselves. An incident occurred outside while the talent show was going on. There wasn't any more room for the rest of those people, so they were trying to push in to see their friends perform anyway they could. We made them leave the school grounds. A couple of individual fights broke out in the auditorium that we immediately took care of. Then there was one incident outside, after the show. Someone was out there shooting, and we had to call the city law enforcement to back us up."

Floyd: "The police did arrest five people that night. After that we saw about twenty crip gangsters coming towards the school and we did what we usually do in a situation like that. We went to the leader for a peace truce. The police came back around and blocked off the streets. It was necessary to make Park Street exit into one way so that we could get the crowd away from the school."

Jackie: "Our security did a good job. It had been a great night and we went back in the building talking about how good our pay was going to be. We went into H.'s office and asked for our money. I couldn't believe it when he said, "What pay? I didn't say I was going to pay you. I said I had a present for you." He stood up and passed us all a Milky Way!"

Benny: "I was thinking about more than a Teachers Association grievance when he gave us that Milky Way. That was his way of showing his resentment by letting us know we weren't worth .50 to him. Then he told us that in spite of what he had promised, our money would appear on our next pay check as overtime pay. That man was sad. That man had a bad problem that let us know that we would never be appreciated by him at all. He seemed jealous of our abilities and crazy as well. In my experience, dope is usually involved when a person acts in such a way as he did. Our job wasn't nearly as dangerous and difficult at that time when Mr. Hawks used to give us bonuses for Christmas, special achievement bonuses, and a bonus for the summer break because he appreciated us. The past principal, Principal Hawks was a good man. Some of the teachers, white ones too, used to invite us out to their houses for dinner in the Heights because they appreciated us. Also I remember one Christmas; they had a potluck at the school in which the school had paid for. Like a totem pole, if it's a fight in the classrooms, we are the first ones they call on to straighten things out.

Anyway, Mrs. Faison and H. got this potluck together that the school paid for. He called all the teachers and other staff together to eat before we ate. I remember they called Mr. Peterson, the Vice-Principal and asked him was he finished eating? I heard H. say, "Wait a minute before you call them up." He went and got some more to eat first. To me, he made it seem like we were extra dogs and we could have the scraps. Our protest was that we refused to eat after that. I did not want to. He made it seem like we weren't worth anything and we are the hardest working people in the building. We always had plenty to eat at my house anyway.

Ha! I'm reminded how on one spring afternoon, we were getting ready to let the buses out to leave for home when some of the students started screaming, "She's got a gun!" I turned around and this girl named Stacy had a 9m.m cocked and up in the air. The other girl she had it in for had a knife. This was something that I'd never seen before in my life. Security Floyd Smith was closest to the one with the knife, so he took the girl by the wrist and kicked with his knee somehow to get the knife from her. In the meantime, Mr. H. had grabbed the girl with the gun by the waist, holding on, which she still could have shot somebody. We were mind boggled when this young girl pulled him, a grown man, from Park Street all the way to the end of the school. She pulled him for at least thirty feet. She and Mr. H. were going to get somebody killed, so I rushed over there and locked her wrist; put a wrist lock on her so she was unable to pull the trigger, and took the gun from her hand. When it was over, she wanted to know if she could get her gun back. Then Mr. Peterson told her, "No!" "No!". Mr. Cloud, the building engineer came and tried to unload the gun and he was about to shoot somebody too. That ungrateful H. called all of us up to his office and said we didn't do our job right. We'd had more than enough of his stuff. Mr. Floyd and I tore into him like a bulldog biting into a cat. He predicted an outcome and he shut up then. Everyone knew that if it hadn't been for us, somebody would have gotten seriously hurt or killed that day."

Floyd: "The girl had told us that the other girl had been picking on her about a month before and we had reported it to Mr. H. We told him, "Don't tell us we didn't tell you about the potential seriousness of this over a month ago."

CHAPTER 28

A Good Year

Benny: "The school year of 1992, we got a new supervisor named Dewayne Hodges. He was a retired deputy from the sheriff's department. He also had been one of my Tae Kwon Do instructors when I was twelve years old. Anyway, he and Montgomery really showed they respected what we did and they learned a lot from us. They took what information they learned from us and included us in professional seminars. It was a great year that year with him at Central. We had someone else there that cared about us, the school, and what we were doing. He was also an inspiration to us and I'm sorry that he's gone. Also this was the year we were trained and certified to use cease and desist pressure point. I was able to use this pressure point technique that year when two girls were fighting and one of them started biting me. I pressed a pressure point behind the girl's ear and she immediately stopped. Now this was something that Hodges showed us after all these years."

Floyd: "A week before school started, we told Hodges some things that we could use in training during the football games. That's when we were really busy and needed to use the techniques we learned in training. Deputy Dewayne Hodges named us the experts on gangs."

Jackie: "Dewayne, to me, also showed care and concern. He came in asking questions. He asked me to be his guidance instead of coming in there cold telling us what we should be doing. I guess he had heard from the neighborhood some of the things that we campus supervisors had done. We noticed that they were more focused on Central High because there were more kids here than anywhere and we were managing to keep things under control. Dewayne showed a lot of respect for what we did and how we worked together. I feel he should have been the director of safety and security."

CHAPTER 29

Business as Un-usual

Floyd: "During the school year of 1992, in the cafeteria at lunchtime, we started noticing how all of the different gangs used to line up down the lockers in the hall. They were the Eastside, the Hill tops, the 8ball posse, the Wolfe street crips, the 23rd street crips, Woodrow crips, 13th street crips, Monroe gang, and Highland court. We had all of them here at Central and more. We would have to get all of the security together early down to the cafeteria because they would try to get rowdy with each other. They would be throwing ice or whatever at each other to get something started. We had a job on our hands trying to keep them from fighting. This went on everyday; but we would be on them like ice on rice-so fast, that they wouldn't be able to fight. Rarely would they get a chance to fight. If they did, our policy was to hit them so hard they would immediately stop."

Benny: "After Mr. Smith said that, I'm reminded there is always a gang problem on every hand. It was the bloods fighting the crips. Then it was the bloods fighting the bloods. Then a mix up happened with the Eastside and the 8-ball posse. We were getting ready to let the buses leave when these guys got to fighting- big time. A guy name Big Mike was fighting the Carlock brothers and I mean, Mike was beating those boys to a puff. I remember Mr. Pete was trying his best to break up the fight, but no way could he handle them. He said they were just too strong. When they saw us coming, they just automatically stopped. We took the Carlock boys to the nurse's station because they were beat up pretty bad. I mean, it started a big rivalry and they would start on the Little Rock streets and bring it back to the school."

Jackie: "This security here at Central meant business. If there was a fight, we would go right in and take care of it. We had to. They knew they had a fight on their hands because they had to fight their way through us. We became like the fantastic five."

Floyd: "I remember one incident where H. tried to demand a student they called Freddie Kruger to do something. He told Principal H. not to put his hands on him. H. reached for him and the next thing we knew Freddie had picked H. up and slammed him to the floor. By the time we made it down to the office, a coach was there and had broken up the battle. We had to escort student Freddie off the campus."

Benny: "After Freddie Kruger beat Mr. H. down, he came to us and said, "I thought you all were my buddies, you didn't come help me!" Maybe he knew how we felt about Mr. H. too."

Jackie: "Once again another year with this H. thing. He wanted to know how we felt about another talent show to raise some money. Even though he didn't pay us cash like he'd promised last time, we received overtime on our payroll, so we did the same routine again as the other talent show."

Floyd: "We were about an hour early for the show this time and we ran into this girl who was a student who said that she was trying to find somewhere to change into her costume. The next thing we knew, she was coming out of the main office with her clothes changed and carrying her stockings in her hand. We looked at each other in disbelief. Now why on earth would she go in the main office to change her clothes? She had told us that she was in the talent show, but we never did see a costume and we don't remember her being one of the acts."

Benny: "I mean it was a huge crowd this time also. We had some of the gang members trying to act up again, but other than that, we had a good night. But, after that night we found out that Mr. H. only turned in $500.00 to the bookkeeper. After that report, downtown did a serious investigation because H. was not supposed to be handling any more money; but was still handling it.

The Bookkeeper started asking us questions about the talent show, again. It had been a packed house. We told the bookkeeper every thing. We told her how much they were charging to get in; and didn't anybody get in free either, because we were watching every entrance that had not been locked for fire safety reasons. I became very concerned about this money coming up missing all the time, especially after the first time. For one reason, H. had changed my lunch time and I happened to be sitting in the campus inn with one of the building engineers when H. came in there. He didn't see us, but I saw him walk behind the table where the lady that's in charge of the campus inn keeps her money. He grabbed him a hand full of money and was getting ready to walk back out the door when he noticed me and the other guy. He looked surprised when he asked us what we were doing in there. We told him we were eating our lunch because this is the time that he had given us. He just said, "Oh!" We went on and finished up our lunch. When we left, he was still over there. After this particular incident, an alarm went off for sure and I started wondering about him more and more.

I started watching H., just observing his behavior like he was one of the students. On several occasions, I saw H. during the hall sweep only give certain students D-hall, which is detention. To let you know what is hall sweep; that's when he would wait until the bell rang, then he'd start counting down to the seconds. Thereafter, if a student was still in the hall when he finished his countdown, they would have to do D-Hall. I observed this one particular female run to him quite often when she was late for class. He would give her a pass. I started thinking something is going on. I just had a feeling. Then I observed him having her cornered off and I would say to myself, *which is not appropriate for him to be up on her like that. Something is wrong.* After that I observed his behavior with another young student and then I knew there was something wrong. Was it my responsibility to tell somebody or hers? One day I was telling this first young lady that she needed to get on in to class. Her response was, "Mr. H. knows how this pussy is."

Floyd: "This young lady that Mr. Johnson is speaking about and another young lady from my neighborhood used to be together all of the time. Also she would walk the girl to class and then run to her own class. One day, I asked the young lady that I know to come here. I asked her why she walked the other girl to class. She said that Mr. H. was paying her to walk her to class (?)"

Benny: "A lot of times when Ms. Bernard came over to the school, she would ask questions about a lot of things. Then they called us to come downtown and questioned us security guards. We found out that H. had blamed us for all the money coming up missing. We hadn't handled any of the money except the one football game! My eyes crossed up. For one thing, I know for myself, as a minister, I fear the Lord too much to steal. And none of us has ever been arrested a day of our lives.

Never! They do a record check on all the employees before they hire you. But here we are being blamed for taking the money; not just some of it, but we are being blamed for all of it. I guess that's because in the academic pecking order, we are the last on the totem pole.

When I went downtown and talked with Ms. Bernard, I told her the truth about everything because we are all honest men and trustworthy. Like the kids say, "I told my draws". But; I remember this lady came in to her office while I was talking to Mrs. Bernard and she had called Mr. Peterson. That gave H. plenty of time to get his lies together. "I also knew that he couldn't be trustworthy anyway, because anytime you pull a handicapped kid down the stairs…If downtown could have seen how he handled this student that couldn't help himself, he would have been fired immediately! This kid was one of our favorite students…and also this silly white kid was doing something and he told me to bring the kid to his office. When I brought him in there, he slapped this kid hard in the face and left a big red mark on his face… and these are just some of the incidents I'm telling you about…When I wrote out a true report and gave it to H., he often said he misplaced it… Right now, today I don't see how he is working with the Little Rock school district and getting away with these things…" I talked.

I remember soon thereafter, Mrs. Bernard came up to me at the school and said, "Mr. Johnson we are getting ready to put H. on leave." I felt so happy like they were giving me a birthday party or something. That night it flashed on the news about Mr. H., the Principal of Central High School was being put on leave. One of the administrators from downtown said that they didn't have any choice but to put him on immediate leave because one of the girl's fathers threatened to come to the school and kill H. if they didn't remove him immediately. Allegedly he had taken his daughter off somewhere and she was pregnant. I believe it. But the next morning, we couldn't believe that there were students out in front of the building protesting. We tried to get them to go into the building to class, but they were saying, "Hell no, we won't go!" And they kept saying it repeatedly. After a while, Mike Peterson came out and talked them into going to class. After that, they wanted to go to the cafeteria and carry it on there.

Floyd: "During that protest, one of the students' parents was there also in the middle of the mix. She was highly upset about H. being put on leave also. She came on in the cafeteria trying to persuade the kids to keep on protesting. Even one of my cousins, Jonathan, was in there. Mrs. Magee said leave him alone! So I let him stay in there protesting. He didn't know any better either. In a situation like this, we would usually just ignore the protesters and allow them to stay until they were ready to leave. Mrs. Swain tried to talk them into going to class. She was acting principal until they filled that spot vacated by Mr. Peterson, Pete. The students talked to her surprisingly bad and she went into a panic. We stepped forward then and told her that we would handle it from here on out. This "protest" went on the whole day. The crowd finally died down and most of them went on home. I don't know why she was so upset regarding Mr. H., but Mrs. Mageed wanted to spend the night there!; she and some of the students. The police told her "No", that it was time to close the school and if they did not leave, they were going to charge them with criminal trespassing. However, they insisted and the police kept warning Mrs. Mageed. When she refused to move on, they arrested her. Some of the students came back up there wanting to spend the night. An officer asked them if they had lost their minds, and what was wrong with them."

Benny: "I know people that we knew from the neighborhood- I mean people that we have known since we were young kids and that had known us all of our lives- some of them turned against us. They said that we were the reason that Mr. H. got terminated. They said that we thought we were better than they were. I mean, all kinds of ignorant things were being said to and about us. And there were all kinds of protesting going on."

Floyd: "Each day, it was our job to walk through the building and check to make sure that there were no doors unlocked to any empty rooms. This particular day, it was a vacant office space on the third floor which we had already checked and made sure that the door was closed and locked. All of a sudden, we passed back by after second lunch period and this same door was unlocked again. We went in and checked it out to find out what staff was now using it. We knew that one of the young men had been in there when we found a used condom on the floor. We didn't like it, but we kind of brushed it off as a one time thing we didn't catch that just happened. It happened again after that day, however. It went on for awhile before we decided to take time out and watch to see how he was getting in there, and talk to the couple before we reported it. One day after second lunch, we locked that door to the vacant office space and set up a stake out. And, Aw, man! It was him! First Mr. H. came with a key into the room. Then one of our secretaries came in. They stayed in there for about thirty minutes. After they left, we went in and there were the condoms..."

Benny: "This time it was a basketball game the school was having. I was standing on the southwest end of the gym when I observed some gang signs being thrown around. Right after that, a huge fight broke out. I mean about a hundred gang members started fighting and people were scattered all over the place trying to get away from it. My first instinct told me not to run up in there, but I went on anyway when a policeman's gun was taken away from him. Floyd and I caught each other's eye, then ran up in the stands and started throwing these guys out of the stands. We were just doing whatever it took to get them to stop. After the fighting stopped in the stands, I saw officer Temple with one of the guys handcuffed. He made it down on the floor with his suspect when another fight broke out. We had to turn right around and get that under control. Then someone announced that the game was canceled. The former coach Fitzpatrick was standing out on the court very upset because of what was going on. I mean it was total chaos on every hand- a basketball game. We assisted the policeman outside because he couldn't handle a guy. Then we pushed the crowd off the campus quickly. I know that if it weren't for us, that night, Mr. Smith and me again, knowledge of our job and our community, somebody would have gotten killed. But we did get that game resolved."

CHAPTER 30

I WITNESS

"This is Security Officer Floyd Smith. In 1993, after we went through the suspension with H. and one parent was arrested for staging a protest inside Central's cafeteria, they held a town meeting in the auditorium. A lot of people and a lot of representatives that were backing H. came to the meeting. Many dignified citizens, so to speak, stood up and talked about how the school board was doing him wrong. Security Officer Ben Johnson spoke and stated that we need the truth! We security officers stuck with the truth. We weren't going to tell nothing but the truth and no one was going to persuade us from speaking anything other than the truth.

While the rally was going on, the Muslim organization had been hired as security for H. They sneaked him in the building to speak to the public about his situation. H. came in and spoke about how honest and upright he was and indicated that he had been framed by one of us. The people applauded what he said and said they would back him. We realized that none of the people knew the truth like we did. The meeting went on for quite a while and I thought about how somebody like Christopher Columbus must have felt when he told them the world was round. I was happy when I saw one of the representatives I grew up with was coming through the door. I asked him if he wanted to know the truth. "You and I grew up in the same neighborhood. We used to play together and we have known each other all our lives; me, you, Jackie and Benny. All you had to do was come to someone you knew would give you the truth about this." He was walking with the Muslim organization and I guess he didn't want to mess up his job, so he didn't want to hear the "truth" that we knew.

Some of the other people I grew up with came into the building. The son of my family's doctor came in. He and his brother came to me and told me that his father said to ask me what was going on. We told them the truth. They listened to us and he said, "Floyd, I've known you all my life. I know you wouldn't tell me this if it was anything less than the truth. We know *you* wouldn't just lie on a person." He and his brother decided that they would not be involved with the people who were rallying behind H., and they left. Thankfully, some of the others came over later on and talked to us after the meeting was over with. But a lot of people and some of the kids started lying and accusing us security officers. All we did was testify later on about what we saw and what we knew, which was mismanagement of the money from the talent shows and the games. I never told the total story of other bad experiences with H."

Benny Johnson: I know after suspecting people in the neighborhood we'd been knowing all our lives and ten and twenty years...They started turning against us; saying we were the cause of Mr. H. being suspended, and we weren't no good, and we thought we were better than they were... Aw! Man we were called all kinds of names. Chaos and hell broke out behind that untrustworthy man. There were a lot of protest and they had a meeting up at the school. Some of the students had mock trials.

There were already allegations from the beginning of the suspension that usually when a school board hears the case, it's already a done deal. It's a matter of getting things finalized, right, but they were just going to go on through with the formality of it. During that time, like I said, there were a whole lot of protest and things. The community was reminded how they had been taken advantage of them for years. However, we decided we were just going to stand because I'm a fighter for the right. I'm a warrior myself. Security Officers Floyd smith, Jackie Fells, Jerome Simms, Jerry Smith; I guess we are all fighters. Even though the kids were upset and angry at us, we just kept on working and working and doing our job. So that's how I'm going to end this segment."

Floyd: "Finally, the school lawyer came to Central, Mr. Freeman. We had known him for a long time from when we went to school there. Mr. Freeman got to investigating things and found out what we knew, when, and how long did we know it. We each gave a statement to him. One day John Walker came up to the school. We had not been called or notified that he was coming for an interview. At the time of his arrival I was helping to train the girl's track team. He came to Central and walked on over to track and field where I was. He and another lawyer wanted to talk to me right then. I told him I wasn't able to talk to him at that time because I was too busy training the team. I had the girls on timer and was doing speed/resistance training. He got very obnoxious with me, saying I talked to the school lawyer and why wouldn't I talk to him? I told him I would talk to him, but I couldn't talk to him right then because I was busy. The girls are all there for their timed workouts. He kept on insisting that I stop what I was doing and talk to him. His personality was bad and I was getting irritated, so I kept on with practicing the girls. I was using a speed resistant monitor that I had to reset, but he just kept on talking and interrupting us. He asked me things like; "Uh what is that for, how do you do this, etc, etc....", questioning about the way I was training them. I mean he got real obnoxious. So he continued to hang around, following me stupid like. Finally, the track meet was over, but he had made me so angry, I refused to give him another statement. I told him that I had already given a statement to the district lawyer and he could get the statement from him. Now, that was the only statement I was going to give."

Ben Johnson: I remembered when John Walker came into the building and started doing his evaluation. He started talking to teachers. Some of the teachers said they felt like he was harassing them. I know of one incident; a former employee. Well, she's still an employee now, but her job title has changed. She said he followed her around the building. He followed her to the bathroom and when she came out, he was standing there waiting on her to come out. Then he came to security. He came to me in particular and tried to get me to change my story. Well, one thing about me, I'm going to tell the truth and I'm going to tell only the truth. I wasn't proud of *him*. And one thing I know: If you lie, you will have to tell one lie after another, after another- black, white or chartreuse. John Walker went to several security officers and they could elaborate more. He was working for H. and he had to get us to change our story. I was told that he called someone up and muffled the telephone and tried to intimidate them. He never did try anything like that with me because he knew what type of person I am. I am a strong, dedicated, Christian person. If he had tried to intimidate me, he knew he would have had more problems.

I'm coming in as a member of the Board of Director of C.T.A., the Certified Teachers Association for security officers.

I was called on one afternoon. I believe I was coming back after my lunch duty when this teacher called me from the main office and told me I had a phone call. I asked her if she would transfer it up to the third floor lounge because that's where I was closest to. When I answered the phone, it was John Walker again and he made this statement: "Mr. Johnson, I heard you might want to change your story." I told him I would get back to him later. I wasn't rude or anything, but I just wasn't able to get back to him later. He did everything to get us to change our minds. But one thing about me, Jackie Fells, Floyd Smith, Mr. Jerry Smith and Jerome Sims is that you could not intimidate us. We are strong men who have to stand up. We have the bruises and injuries to prove how we know how to stand up to bigger challenges than this. We are the school's security guards and that's why I am standing on the truth. When I preach, I preach the truth. I know he went above and beyond the call of duty to try to get us to change our mind, but we wouldn't give an inch. Also, after that incident, he had several other lawyers working with him at the law firm. He would send them by and they would ask me different questions backwards and forwards. I know the reason for that was to see if we could change our story. I know he had several people working for him that would try harder and harder to get us to change our mind. But, like I say, we never did budge. We just stood on the word."

"Mr. John Walker approached me, Jackie Fells, about 6pm that evening and made a comment that we shouldn't do Mr. H. like that. He said that we were black, back-stabbing him. Well, if it's true that we are black folks, and we are. As far as being black folks, we should all stick together and it won't make any difference if someone tells a lie on someone else or not? So, let's work together on the truth. Did I say that right?"

"Yeah, yeah, uh huh"(Other security)

I just told him he should get out my face and go on. He had all the information he needed. I sort of felt like Mr. Walker was a predator trying to feed off the security officers to get what he wanted; any mistakes, whatever edge he could get even though Mr. H. was guilty of the crimes. He was just trying to make himself look good as a lawyer which, I guess all lawyers do."

"Ben Johnson again coming in after Jackie Fells again, Board of Directors of Security Officers here at Central High School. I remember right before the board meeting, we went down to the sitting room with Janet Bernard and Byron Freeman, the school district lawyer. They had prepared us a good meal. I mean it wasn't any scraps. I remember I had just had a tooth extracted that night before and I couldn't eat any of it. But they had different kinds of Barbeque, potato salad, slaw salad, sweet beans, good breads, cold drink... I remember Jackie, Floyd and Jerry and all of them, eating real good back there. They were meddling me- my good friends (ha), because I couldn't eat at the time.

For the meeting, I wasn't really jealous, or intimidated, or anything like that, but I saw all the notable people out there who were supporting him and I didn't think I was anybody. I was just standing on the word and I was just telling the truth. And when I sat down to be cross-examined by John Walker, he tried to get me all mixed up. I stood on the truth when he asked me certain things about the money. I didn't quibble or maybe. I told him about the money we collected for the foot ball game and I told him about the talent show. He said, "Was downstairs full?" He was trying to say that people got in free. Did not one person get in free. Still to this day I do not believe that any one person got in free. We had all doors either locked or covered by one of us, and police were monitoring and coming back and forth down stairs. Attorney Walker continued to ask me certain questions like that. Also he asked me questions like was the top of the stands full? He was surprised when I also told him exactly how many people were up there. He asked me, "Mr. Johnson are you sure? No one got in free?" I said, "Sir, I am positive that no one got in free." Even when they pushed their way toward the front door, we pushed them back because we are a security team that works together. I remember that when I got through testifying, it just didn't bother me anymore. I really felt good. He said he didn't have any further questions for this witness. He asked his other attorney if I would need to be recalled. Walker's attorney said, "No". I didn't need to be recalled because he saw that I was standing firm on what I believed in."

"Mr. Walker asked me about the same questions that he asked Benny; about how many people had broken through the line during the talent show. I told him that not one got in. Mr. Smith, Mr. Benny Johnson and I, **Jackie Fells**, controlled the crowd. We got everybody settled down and continued to sell the tickets to a full capacity crowd. The tickets were sold for $5 a head. The problem was Mr. H.'s, plain and simple. He turned in a lesser amount of money than was collected that night. I explained it to him. One question he asked me about was did I ever walk into H.'s office. I told him, "Yes." He asked me to explain that to him. I told him I walked into the office to see Mr. H. with a pillow case full and piles of money on top of his table. And yes, he had at least three other females in there counting the money and there was a lot of money. Then he asked me questions about the parking lot area; "Was it packed?" I told him, "Yes." Then he asked me pretty much the same questions he had asked Benny. So I will allow him to elaborate on that end."

Benny: "After Mr. Walker finished asking me questions, he told me I could step down, and then he said; By the way, I need to recall Mr. Fells because he knows some allegations about some women in the building. He was suggesting that the women also stole the money."

Floyd: "During the hearing down at the school board, the day we all were supposed to meet, I guess all of the witnesses for the district met in the back. I spotted a few of the girls that went to Central and found out that these were some of the girls that had written allegation statements about him messing with them. While the trial was going on, the school district lawyer was also questioned and he brought in witnesses that were questioned. Then John Walker questioned them after the school district lawyer questioned those witnesses. It went on and on. When it came time for me to come out, they asked me to sit down and allow the school district lawyer to interrogate me first. He asked me a bunch of questions pertaining to the talent show, the tickets, and the money that was collected during the foot ball game. I described to him how we ran our set up: One security would flag the car in, one would take the money and put tickets on the car window. We would then park all the cars. Once we got them parked, we would wrap the tickets and the money up together in order. After we filled the parking lot, we would call H. and turn all the money and tickets over to him. I described to him how we had that set up.

Then the school district lawyer asked me about the talent show. I described how we moved around at the talent show, what went on and what we observed: We had some parents helping to collect money for admissions to the show while H. was standing at the table with a big beige sack. He put the money into the bag. Then he would run out of that little lobby, run down the hallway, and run inside his office. We could hear his door open, heard him dump the money off, shut his door, then run right back out to us. I told everyone how he would do that. I described to everyone what we were hearing that night. Then he asked me did or could anybody have gotten in there without paying. I told him, "No", because we had custodians downstairs also keeping an eye on people in case someone tried to sneak in. We had locked the doors with chains on the backs of them down below, and we had gates in between the halls to cut the hallway off away from the event. We had them shut off and shut out, so no one got in free. The school district lawyer said he had no further questions."

Jackie: "It wasn't attorney John Walker, it was the other lawyer on the John Walker team who questioned me and he kind of asked me the same things. I confirmed the same things that I told the school district lawyer; that no one got in free. The way we ran the parking lot setup, the way we wrapped the money up and gave it to H., the talent show; how no one could have possibly gotten in free because of how well we ran security. I repeated about how downstairs had standing room only in the auditorium and that upstairs had at least three hundred people up there. He finally let me go. After I stepped down off the chair and returned to the back, I saw that some of the girls that made accusations about him were afraid. John Walker had intimated some of the other people on the stand which made some of the girls upset. They were crying and didn't want to go up there. That is what I noticed in the back after I left and had finished getting questioned."

Benny Johnson: "Yes, they called some kids to the stands and the kids made allegations that we weren't trustworthy, we smoke dope, we get high, try to take their girlfriends, we didn't do our jobs and were just no good in general. You know, they tried to discredit us in every way possible and make us look real bad. Fortunately, some of the people there really knew the truth. Even Mr. John Walker, as quiet as it was kept; I could tell that he even knew the truth and what was going on. But, for some reason, some of the kids got up there and started telling a whole bunch of lies. I remember coming back to school and this one young lady started cursing and said we were lying on them. I hurried up and sent her to the office for what she was trying to do. She was trying to get a bunch of kids together and form a mob and let it get out of control. I immediately took her to the office where they suspended her. I mean she started cursing, and I mean, just very out of order-like she had been staged. After that incident and she got suspended, it didn't take long for it to just die out. And I can really say this and I can say this from my heart; that a lot of times when black people get upset and decide to do something about some things, they will do it for a while, then it will all die out. This is another good example of that; that it will just all die out. A lot of this was media stunts. And for a lot of people, it was just for self-glory, anyway. But, like I say, some important things just die out."

Jackie Fells: After all the district's witnesses went up, John Walker started presenting his witnesses. Of all the witnesses that went up, one in particular we were curious about. She was supposed to be testifying on behalf of the district, but she evidently had changed her story. From what we heard, she is the one who turned this information in to the district in the first place. After the girl who made accusations went towards her, she came up as a H.'s character witness. We were all looking surprised because I found that kind of strange, you know. That if she is the one who turned this information in to the district, then why was she testifying on his behalf? Then after she testified, it got crazy.

Some of the kids they put up on the stand started saying a lot of stuff that wasn't true about my coworkers that I've known for years. They accused us of messing around with the girls there. I knew that wasn't true. We all have good wives and relationships our own age. They accused us of selling dope on campus and that wasn't true either about any of us or my coworkers. All of it was false, and all of it was new information I had never heard before. They created accusations trying to discredit us. As hard as we work to keep this school safe and under control, people would let these kids get up there and try to discredit us like they did was unbelievable. They just got up there and made up accusations off the wall about things that didn't have any facts about anything. Stories that we were doing this like and we were like that... Like I said, none of the accusations they made toward me or my coworkers had any facts about nothing."

Benny: "I recall an incident one evening I didn't tell anybody because I didn't think it was my place to tell. I recall one evening that I was walking to the office about 4p.m. When I saw a young lady in the office who was looking very sad, I asked her was something wrong? But she wouldn't say anything. I kept on talking to her trying to make her feel better, but then she started crying. She finally opened up and told me something that was extremely disturbing. Her principal had walked up on her and grabbed her genitals, grabbed her around the back, and asked her if she liked how that feels. I asked her, "What did she do, what did she say?" She had told him, "No sir, I don't like how that feels. Stop, and Leave me alone."

I became very embarrassed, very ashamed that she had called him sir like that. And while she was sitting there, I said a prayer and told her didn't she think she ought to tell somebody? She said right now she was too scared, but she was thinking about it. Later on, she did present that information to one of the vice principals. As Mr. Smith stated earlier; that he saw several girls in the back room crying and she had been one of them. It wasn't the fact that she was so nervous about what was going on in the courtroom. She was nervous about what her friends and everyone else who was a student here would think. Would she look bad herself, or would they think she was trying to make up a lie against Mr. H. that was the truth?"

"Sheesh! I think that the school district was very lenient with Mr. H. considering all the things he did to us here. I am Mr. **Fells** and I recall the time he accused me of taking drug money for the students. Out of the blue, he had me suspended, like he just needed to get rid of me. I was on suspension for almost three months before someone came to their senses. I won my case and was repaid back money and some extra before I could start back working again. Really, the school board just patted Mr. H. on his back and sent him a free ticket out of here because they were scared of all the legalities and probably all the publicity to enforce the issues against him. He hurt a lot of people. He was not a good man."

Benny Johnson: "Yeah, I'm, coming right after Jackie Fells and I'm recalling during the trial downtown at the Board, a teacher here, I am not going to use her name, would leave out of her room. And you know it's the school rules that you shouldn't leave your class unattended. She would leave her room looking for Mr. H.. "Where's Mr. H.. Where's Mr. H.?" She would walk from 16th Street to 14th Street and from the basement to the top floor, the 4th floor, trying to find Mr. H.. It was alleged that they were dating anyway. And she was one of his supporters. She was, in my opinion, a big instigator around here after the H. trial got to rolling along. She was going around collecting some of the other teacher's support. I never saw so many of the same faculty so divided among each other. Even though they knew he was guilty, some of them still wanted to support a man that was guilty and messing around with the young students. You know that takes a sorry type of person who would just support someone they know is guilty of those types of crimes. That's just to show you how society is now today."

Floyd: "After the hearing, I recall stepping outside for some air and a couple of the parents that I knew were out there. One of them I spoke to after I got off the stand told me; "You know now Floyd, this is just making you all look like a fool." I told her can't nobody make me look like a fool if I'm up there telling the truth. If anyone wants to call me a fool for telling the truth, then they must be a fool for not wanting to hear it. And that was my comment to this parent. She was a big supporter of H.'s, but like I explained to her that regardless of what they might say about us- No. All we did was go up there and tell the truth to the best of our ability, which we knew was the truth, which was all of the truth."

Benny: "I can recall a time when a couple of parents approached me and said "How are you all letting the white folks manipulate us and get us caught up against a great man such as H. is. I told them that it was no way in the world I was brought up to worship anybody except God. For some crazy reason, I always thought the whole point for everybody was for us to be security in the building. And that is what security is for: to secure, to protect and to serve this school. Whoever is found doing wrong, we are supposed to report that. You aren't supposed to lie about it. Some of the privacy language I heard between him and a female teacher..., Oh, it was a shameful situation."

"This is security officer Jackie Fells again. I can recall the times when I'd work after school, I observed some of the teachers bringing dinner to Mr. H.'s office. And they would stay up there for an hour or two. He made good dates. That's something that I was always told. He got so much attention from many different females in the building. Some of them were married teachers. And I was just wondering why they couldn't see it- a skunk like that."

CHAPTER 31

On and On, on the Up and Up

"This is Officer Ben Johnson again. I can remember when the hearing came to an end; the School Board took a while to make a decision. The decision was to not re-negotiate H.'s contract, and that he would have to find another job somewhere else. I know that after the hearing was over, and from what we heard during that summertime, that it was a package deal done. The meaning of this was that if H. goes, then everyone knew the security guards were innocent. However, the security guards would have to go also. More than likely, they would reassign us. That's how life is. I can recall the director of security calling me up and saying Benny we're going to have to do some changes, man. He said it politely. "You are going to have to go to another school." I said, "Wait a minute. You know how I am. Where did this come from?" He said well, we're just going to have to make some changes." That's all he said. I said, "You're going to have to explain to me more than that!" So I immediately called Frank Martin with the Union, the executive president for the CTA.- Certified Teachers Association.

They ignored rules of fair play in that they wanted us away from Central High School because they thought we were a problem now that we had reported the real problem. But he called me back after the CTA contacted him. I guess it took about a week. Even the teachers were mad. Even the teachers had called downtown. We had some big supporters here who voiced their opinions that they wanted us to stay in the school. Some of them said that if we weren't in the schools, they weren't going to be back either. They were going to stay out and let some scabs come in because that's how much support and respect we had around Central High School. They knew we kept a good and safe environment. They *knew* we kept it as safe as we could without it turning into a prison or military zone.

It was around about that time then that Mr. Rudolph Howard came in to make some big changes. He wanted all the security gone. That was going all around the school. So, I just watched him and really observed him to see what was going on. It appeared to be true. I had to believe it when he started writing up reports on me that weren't all the way true. He began making up things and reporting half truths against me. Immediately, I contacted the Classroom Teachers Association again about that. Once he had written that I wasn't on my post and that I was late on the job all the time, which was a bold face lie. Oh boy, he began by making up a lot of things to get rid of us. But he didn't know me. We'd been through too much to just be railroaded like this. I went and got some teachers to type up and Xerox some things for me, and got a petition started. They showed me that I did my work well. Every last one of the teachers on the first floor and north end of the building wrote on the petition to the Certified Teachers Association, not that I did my job, but that I did it well; that they appreciated me, respected my work and complimented me highly."

Floyd: "O.K. like Rev. Johnson stated so well, it finally came to a head. Over the summer we started hearing accusations that some changes ought to be made at the school by transferring the security officers. We heard that we had a new principal coming in and that it was a package deal that Mr. Howell would get rid of the old security at Central with his coming. He believed the superintendent and Ms. Bernard would have to leave the district. Come the next year, we found out that this occurred after they found and hired a new superintendent. They didn't hire a new superintendent at that time, however. Ms. Bernard was in charge of the school district. Yeah. We heard accusations coming from everywhere that they were going to get rid of us. Finally, the new school year started and we got a new principal. This next year, we also got a new resource officer. We later discovered that he was an undercover officer. Word had gotten around about the accusations that some of the kids had made about us; that we were dope heads, selling dope on campus and messing with the young female students. And they wanted to make sure this wasn't true, which I don't blame them. Anyway, he was the one sent here to keep an eye on us. He did not know it, but we also kept an eye on him. Important friends would contact us or our family members to let us know all the stuff going on downtown- what were the changes, why, and things like that. They told us this officer was put in place here indefinitely. Officer Hart was sent here to keep an eye on us. He was sent here to investigate the accusations against us, write us up at every opportunity, and get rid of us for that year. We decided what we would do was just do our job. If we did our job like we were used to doing- telling the truth, doing our job, we already had the support of the whole faculty."

Rev. Benny: "Rudolph Howard came to try to feel security out. We already knew he was told to get rid of us. He really didn't know any better. Lots of people didn't know any better. However, we knew the problem was over when he called us in a meeting and told us we weren't the bad people some people had led him to believe after all. He was fascinated and said he really enjoyed working with us. He ended up giving us high compliments. I enjoyed working with him also. We got along real well.

But as the year went on it, some things-disciplinary problems with some kids got worse and worse. I was used to working with kids, but it was something going on, in the air, on television, or something that was making the kids worse. They were becoming more rude, angry and disrespectful. As a member of Board of Director of C.T.A., I went down to the board meeting and told them to let Mr. Rudolph Howard do his job with the disciplining of students. I came back to school the next day and Mr. Howard pulled me to the side. "Come, come over here", he said. He didn't want anyone else to overhear the conversation. I told him I did it for the school. I spoke up for the security measures. If some of the kids were fighting, they needed to be suspended. I was referring to a couple of incidents. I remember some kids went scott free, you know, and continued to walk around the campus. Several guys had jumped on this one individual and just one of them was suspended. I got real upset about that for the safety of all of the students here. I didn't want anybody to get hurt or killed under our watch. Mr. Howard said, "Well, you be careful when you go downtown with what you say because you are definitely telling the truth. But, what you say falls back on me." I said, "Well Mr. Howard, you had your house nigger and you had your field niggers. I said, "Are you a house nigger?" His remark was, "I aint *no* house nigger." At the time, we laughed about that, but I guess I've never been careful about what I say."

Floyd Smith: "After all the trouble that we went through with the H. era, everything finally settled down and they brought a new principal in by the name of Mr. Rudolph Howard. He had to come and get the school back in order with the help of the security officers. Benny had his back, I guess you could say, and everything was calm. Everybody went to school, enjoyed school and we were happy again. At the end of that first year, I thought everything was peaceful. Mr. Howard called the security guards into his office and told us one of the reasons he had been sent to the school was to get rid of the security officers. They weren't doing their jobs right, they were misbehaving; they were fooling around inappropriately with the girls. Mr. Howard had to come and apologize for that. He found that to be untrue. He found that we were about business and we meant what we did on the job in reality. We sat there with him and talked for quite a while. Actually, we were appalled to hear what he mentioned about how lousy a job we were supposedly doing here, but he gave us great credit for the job he now saw that we did. He asked us to continue a job well done. We could ask him for whatever we needed and he told us not to worry about a thing. I appreciated him for what he had done this year."

CHAPTER 32

Black and Blue

Floyd Smith: "So when principal Rudolph Howard was sent to get rid of us, he found out that we weren't the people that some people had discredited us to be. He discovered how serious we were in doing our job especially one day during lunchtime in the cafeteria. Instead of it being a peaceful time to eat and relax with your friends, lunchtime became the hardest and most dangerous part of the day. We really had to work down in the cafeteria. We had a whole lot of gang problems there. We had the East Ends, Eight Balls, Woodrow Crips, Wolfe St. Crips, 23rd St. Crips, you name it; all in there together. East End used to go to Hall High. The principal over there, Dr. Anderson used to work downtown and he was over student assignments. When he became principal of Hall High, someone changed the student zoning there so that most of the east end kids now had to attend Central. That became our biggest problem at Central. We had to jump in the middle of fights between gang members. During lunch times, gangs would be lined up along the lockers. Our security team had to show dominant force many times down in the hallway outside the cafeteria to keep the gang members from starting fights out there, and keeping it cool everywhere else. They had to know that if a fight broke out, we were going to win the battle. Jerome, Benny, Jerry, Jackie and myself; we were going to win the battle.

And this was the first action Mr. Howard had ever seen like this. A fight broke out and a bunch of kids came running by him. He held out both of his hands for them to stop; telling them to stay back in order to keep them away from becoming involved in the fight. But did they listen to him? They just ran right past him. At the time he was the only one down there. When he had gone down there, there was just a couple of us security in the cafeteria. The rest of us got called in from inside the hallways. He saw how we had to come in there and cleared house. When we got there, most of the kids just backed off when they saw us coming. They knew that we could get physical because we had to with these guys. We physically broke them up after we fought our way through the crowd. This wasn't just on a few occasions anymore. Any day of the week during lunch time this would break out because so many different gang members had all been sent to Central. Most of the time it would be really rough until we could weed them out and get to suspending them.

Mr. Howard got to the point where he said, "Bring them to my office!" He started suspending them left and right. I'm sending them off and shipping them away from here. If they all want to fight at Central; they can't fight somewhere else?! But, I want them to understand they are not going to fight here!" He was angry at the situation that had been given to him. Like the new kid on the block, at that point, he found out how much he needed us there and how important the regular security guards were at Central. I don't believe that they'd know the job we had to do at Central. Couldn't any other security officers in the district do what we had to do; know how to do things the way we had to do them? Not even the policemen could come in there and do the job that we did on a regular basis at Central. They didn't have the knowledge of the gang member operations as we did. We had grown up in the community and we knew many of the kids and their families. Principal Howard found out someone hadn't told him the truth about us. Just like the guy said, "Hey, these guys don't have time to run around and do nothing bad because they are too busy just keeping this school under control." I mean it was just like running a prison at times."

Floyd Smith: "One day during another lunch period, I spotted some guys from the East End throwing gang signs up. They have symbols they display with their fingers and hands. This guy who was a Crip was walking along and they tried to cut him off for a gang beating. I caught up with them quick and took them to the Vice Principals office. I told him what they were trying to do and he sent them straight home. I returned to the cafeteria where lunch was still going on. When I got down to about the middle of the cafeteria, these two guys approached me. One of them walked behind me and the other one stepped in front of me and asked me, "Now, what's up now- punk?" Suddenly, this kid swung at me. I managed to block his punch and slap him on side of the neck on a nerve I had learned in Tai Kwon Do training. He flew backwards toward his crowd. Just about that time I turned around, this other guy, a gang member from the East End, rushed me from behind. Adrenaline started pumping and before I knew it, I had picked his body up. Coach Boone was in there and came running over. I was about to slam him when coach Boone caught his feet some kind of way. He blocked his feet and was yelling, "Oh Lord, not the floor, not the floor, Floyd!" I caught myself, turned around and threw him on one of the cafeteria tables.

Even as I was walking away from the guy, the other one kept charging me again and again. I grabbed him in an elbow lock and had to slam him into the floor to make him stop. I got up and I walked away from that one. By that time, someone had called in a code three that there was a fight in the cafeteria. But I had kept on walking away from the guys after I had to throw them. I don't punch children. Then the other one got up off the table and he charged me. I grabbed him by the neck and threw him down on the floor. By that time, Jackie Fells had made it on in there by diving through the crowd. He grabbed the guy; the one that I slammed on the table earlier and pinned him down. And now the other guy, after I had slammed him, had gotten back up and was charging me. Jerry Smith dove through the crowd and had to wrestle him into one of the columns real hard. You could hear the thump. It was a fierce thump everywhere: BOOMP! But he gets back up and looks at his other gang members from the East End and asked them, "Is y'all gonna help?" "What!, I thought. Are we going to have to go on and beat the daylights out of these guys before they quit?" Fortunately, those other guys just looked at him. They all shook their heads and stepped back and said, "You two started it, so you're on your own now." Jerry let him go, and he just slumped down to the floor. Jerry had stopped him just in time. They had had plans for me. At the same time, Jackie still had this guy pinned on the floor while I was walking away. I tried to walk out of the cafeteria to get cleaned up and clear my head, but this other guy came right back at me! I grabbed his wrist and put him in a wrist lock. He was still trying me, so I finally had to slam him into the column there also.

When Officer Hart finally came over there, it seemed like officer Hart was upset with me for defending myself. The first thing he said was, "I got him, Floyd" and asked *me* to let him go! - You know, after he just now appeared. And I just looked at him carrying on like he was protection from this monster who liked to beat up on kids.

I went upstairs to Mr. Peterson and told him what happened. Mr. Peterson called 911 even though officer Hart was already there. Mr. Peterson called a police patrol car to come to the school and do the report because I don't know if Mr. Peterson thought officer Hart would write an objective report at that time. All I know is Hart didn't do the official report. Then Mr. Peterson told me to take off the rest of the school day, go to the prosecuting attorney's office and file charges against the young man for attacking me. I left the school that day and went and pressed charges against that particular gang member- the first one that attacked me. They kicked him out of school and neither guy was allowed to return to Central anymore. I was pretty upset about that whole deal; but, those guys had tried to jump me and really do me harm. I had to defend myself against them to the best of my ability so that I wouldn't get hurt or killed. The reason that guy had tried to do me in is because I stopped them from starting a gang war in the high school cafeteria."

Jerry: "Yeah we had an incident with the East Side player's gang, as they called themselves. Their bus used to arrive late. Coach Calloway would be inside the auditorium. And when that bus would be on time, they wouldn't go to class after all. When they didn't go to class, we put all the late students in the auditorium. Coach Calloway had to assign them all Detention (D hall). Sometimes a possible hundred or more would be in his line. At that time they would come to school and hang around in groups of twenty or thirty some young men- you name it. The east end gang would hang out like that. So, we had to keep a close eye on them. They would walk up and down the hallway in groups with a mob mentality. As they walked, we kept tabs on them. Whoever was in that zone, we called ahead so that they would know their location and to keep an eye out for them. That's how we had to keep them from doing something; we sat on them. To me, it seemed like they would only come to school everyday to purposely jump people who were not from the east end's gang. If there wasn't any security around and they came across one of the other gang members who weren't from the east end, the majority of the time they would jump them. And they got to a point they had beaten some people up pretty bad. It kept going on. We tried to stop it, but it really kept going on. They had it out against one of the biggest gangs in our school called the Eight Balls."

Floyd:"We knew most of those guys and we would always talk to them about it saying, "You all need to keep your cool in school, now. Don't get to fighting up in here because you know we're going to get involved and you will all be suspended." East end said they didn't care. Every opportunity they got the chance, they would jump someone in the eight balls. Another significant incident happened with one of the East End gangs down in the cafeteria. They finally got a chance to jump "Big Blue". (Big Blue, God rest his soul, died in 2004 at the wrong place at the wrong time during an attempted robbery. It was proven that he had been converted away from gangs and had not been involved.)

His gang was then called the Woodrow Crips. Background information is that Woodrow Crips and Wolfe St and 23rd St. were on the HBO Special "Banging in Little Rock". They just had it in for the guy. But, they put up a fierce battle. I wouldn't say they lost. I wouldn't say they won; but by the time we could get to them, boy, they were battling! About ten guys tried Big Blue. They tried hard to follow him up the steps and Big Blue would punch them on the chin. Guys would buckle to their knees down the steps. They kept trying to follow Big Blue up to the third floor center stairs. Blue turned around swinging and knocked this one guy flat out down the steps. Then another tried to come up the steps behind him. Big Blue swung and knocked that one down the steps. A third one came up on him and he quick punched that one-knocked down the steps. We had to climb over several bodies Big Blue had knocked out cold to get to him.

By the time we met up with "Blue" there was about five of them against one and they were having a time trying to put him down. We broke it up and put those five in Rm 125, the Study Hall Room. We tried to clear the hall out, but we still had these ten guys trying to get down the hall; trying to get him. But they had a problem. They couldn't get past us. And those guys kept talking real tough. It was only like five of the original Woodrow crips left. But this one guy, a little short guy who was the leader there, was still talking tough. So, I said, "O.K. You don't want to leave; you want to get at them? O.K." I picked out five. I said, "You five go on in there and get them and Big Blue if you can." But no, just like I thought, they didn't want to go in there five on five; they wanted to go in there 40 on five. I told him, "Naw! No way! We say, you all are not going to get in there!" The little guy decided that it was best that they went on away about their business.

We got with them and Big Blue and the other ones that were involved. We had to write them all up and send them home for a while. That was just a few of the problems we had with gang problems. Sadly, it got worse before it got better. Although he had been a gang leader, Blue was a good person and became somewhat of a legend in the community."

Jerry Smith: "We also had it to happen that problems happening outside of the school would trigger over into the school. If they went to the movies, or a party or anywhere else that these gang members would meet, it was always a big fight.

I can remember after Hart had been working with us for just a little while, he saw that we weren't the people that some had accused us of being. He saw that there was too much work going on for us to do to have enough time to engage in the corruption we had been accused of. Some people had gotten on the witness stand and testified to what was supposedly being said that was going on among the security guards. Officer Hart had gotten on the bandwagon and said, "I'll keep watch on these bad guys by working with them."

CHAPTER 33

My Friend Benny

Floyd Smith: "It finally got to the point where Benny Johnson just got fed up with what was going on. He didn't think they were suspending enough of these kids when they should have. So, unfortunately for us, he resigned. Benny was resigned from Central for only one week, though. Within the week that he resigned, we decided that we all were going to take a few days off, get some rest, and let them bring in some substitutes to do our job. So, all of us security guards, the regular ones-Benny was already on leave, temporarily quit. We took off that day for some r & r. evidently, the press got a hold to the fact that none of the security showed up for work at Central High School the next day. The press thought we were protesting.

We found out later on that one of the students came to school and discovered that the regular security guys weren't there. He told his friends and then called his parents to come and get him. They all went out and got to calling and going to the attendance office calling their parents en masse. Their parents began checking their children out of school left and right because the regular security guards were not there. They were not going to let their kids stay at that school without them. This is how safe they felt with us. Even though we had the biggest main gangs were here at Central, they knew they would be safe as long as we were there. A huge check out problem went on that morning. It got to the news media and the school was in chaos. People started calling my house asking me what was going on. The students did not trust new people coming in, nor did the teachers trust anyone except the regular security guards to know how to do the job at Central.

They knew that no other security knew how to do the kind of work we had to do at Central. And right now today, it's the same way. There are some good security officers in the district, but it's very few that can do the kind of job we were doing up at Central. It was hard to explain this to people who weren't there. For one reason, we had learned to work as a team. All the little things we found out that happened outside of the school, we had to be up and share that information with each other. If someone sneezed funny, we had to be up on that too because it could mean anything to another gang member. We became experts on gang signs and how they wore their hat, how they wore their clothing and who was who in their rank. We had to know anything and everything because these days it could cost someone their life. We had to throw them off with periodic searches. If we didn't do that and a weapon showed up from somebody's locker, anything could happen. Kids were getting killed. These kids were now bringing guns to school. They were hiding knives. They were bringing dope and paraphernalia. They were bringing anything that shouldn't have been on a school campus was there. It was dark years for the school district with the gang problem. This is when it really hit rock bottom.

A lot of times, it wouldn't be that long before we'd be reading in the paper or hearing it on the news about one of our kids; how somebody had gotten shot or killed. It was an epidemic these days. Little Rock was having over 40 deaths a year of teenagers. The gang problem had gotten to that point. The majority of these kids were guys that we had to deal with on a regular basis at Central High. And if they didn't go to our school, we had to deal with them at some of the athletic games. Like I made the statement again; this was our job and it was rougher than being in the army or marines. It was like war but worse because we were fighting with children."

Ben Johnson: "In the end of this year I got very frustrated. I had trouble sleeping at night. I got frustrated at Mr. Rudolph Howard, the principal at the time. And he had jumped up in the air and said, " I ain't no house niggah!" And man I didn't know it, but he started pouting. Children were getting beat up. I mean I had never seen anything like it. 15 to 20 boys would jump on 1 or 2 kids and nothing would happen to them. I mean, I'm just concerned about the safety of the school. But, it just kept going on and on. I talked to Mr. Howard and Ms. Russo, who was the vice-principal then about it. She is a principal now. She would take the kids, these rich white kids into her office. She would take up for them. I saw this. While Coach Calloway would be in the auditorium making detention slips up, the other kids; rich white kids would say, "I'm going to Ms. Russo's office." The next thing I'd know, they'd run off to Ms. Russo's office and get an excused pass to class while black kids or the middle class white kids would get an assignment to Detention Hall. I thought that was very unfair and I told them so. It started getting around-"I'm going to Ms. Russo's office." It got to the point if you wrote a kid up, it didn't mean anything. There wasn't any discipline in the school. It was sad.

I went to Mr. Howard and tried to talk to him again. He said, "Mr. Johnson, Uhuh." He said, "Downtown won't let me do anything." And I just got totally fed up. But, the straw that broke the camel's back was down in the cafeteria one day. I'll never forget it! About 15 guys jumped on this one kid. I mean they beat the kid to a pulp before we could get to him. They messed him up. The kid couldn't even walk. He was beat up in that bad a shape on a school campus. The very next day, I stopped these same kids when I saw them circling another one. I went to Mr. Howard and said, "Mr. Howard, what is going on? I mean all these guys jumped this one boy and all of them are back to school today except for one of them. I say what is going on?" He shook his head and said, "There's nothing I can do." He either couldn't or wouldn't give me an explanation.

He made me very, very upset. I'm man enough to say that kid's beating had made me cry that night. I mean, me sacrificing myself at the board meeting because I cared about what was going on wrong at the school. I just got so frustrated, I told Mr. Howard; "I'm leaving. I am resigning today and I ain't coming back here because this is not right. You all are going to get somebody's child killed up in here- right here, up inside this school!" He just said, "Mr. Johnson, don't Benny!...", but he didn't look back at me.

After that, I was so angry I got sick. My blood pressure shot up, but I went to State of Arkansas Restaurant down on 12th Street and called the media and set up a press conference. I told them exactly why after all these years, I had quit my position. I went on live on Channel 4. I told the public I had resigned and I told them what was going on in the school. I told them how we had one black boy who was found to have some crack cocaine on him. He was expelled from school, but we caught someone else with a pouch full of powdered cocaine which is more expensive and more potent. They said all he needed was rehab and he was back in school the next day. He was white. The other kid who was African American got arrested first, and then expelled. I told them I just resigned that day because I was tired of it all and I wasn't putting up with it no more.

Even after I resigned, I still went on down to the board meetings to let the board know what was going on in the schools. I'll never forget Ms. Gee, she was a board member at the time. She called me over after a board meeting one night and said; "Benny. You enjoy the work you do. You work real well with kids and I like you. But, she said, "Benny, do you ever have anything good to say about it all?" I said, "Honestly, no, not at this time. Too many bad things are continuing to go on and the people need to know what is really going on." I went to several other board meetings and after I got through talking, Ms. Poindexter said, "Ben, I am very sorry to hear that you have resigned." She was the President of the School Board at the time. Presently she is a State Representative. Her name is Chesterfield now. She said, "I just wish you would pray on it and consider coming back to the district because you are an asset to this school district. You are instrumental because you care about the kids, you care about the job and I am asking that you think about it." At that time, Dr. Henry Williams had a writing pen in his hand and he threw it down in anger when he heard her ask me to return.

So, I prayed about it and told my wife, who thought about how I couldn't help at all if I wasn't there. I would be starting over at another job that might have some of the same problems or worse. Very shortly after that day, I decided to just report back to work at Central one morning. Mr. Peterson met me in the hallway and said, "Mr. Johnson, I need you to come into my office." I followed him to his office and he told me that Dr. Henry Williams, the superintendent needed to see me downtown. I went and got Frank Martin, one of our union executive presidents to go downtown with me as a witness. We met with Mr. Gadberry and superintendent Henry Williams. Mr. Williams said, "Mr. Johnson, you have resigned and I do not want you back in that place because it seems like you are unhappy." I said, "O.K. that won't be a problem." He said, "Henderson Middle School needs some help out there." Later, I found out Mr. Williams went out there to the school and had a meeting with some of the Crips and Bloods. These kids had told him, "You are on our turf now, and you need to leave our building." He left there and told the principal, "Man, you all need a lot of help out here." That is why he asked me to go out there to Henderson because they were having a whole lot of problems. With my experience and with my physique, my presence would help keep order in their school. So I said, "That is fine. I think I will enjoy going out there. But, before I leave your office, Mr. Williams, there is something that I have to say to you. I brought Mr. Martin here as a witness. I heard that this is your way of keeping me quiet or to secretly get rid of me. I saw you at the school board meeting. But please understand that I also know what you tried to do. If you continue to connive and try to do illegal stuff to me, I am going to a lawyer." OOH, he got hotter than fish grease. Man his eyes turned red. Then I told him, "I am trying to help and you should just leave me alone."

Man, when I walked out of his office, he looked like he may would have had a heart attack. I always thought he was the lousiest superintendent the school district ever had, though. I left there and the next day, I reported to Henderson Middle school. And when I got there I said to myself, "What in the world have I gotten myself into. I was jumping out of a skillet into a fireplace."

Floyd: "So after Ben left the school this day, we were worn out. The security officers decided together that day that we were going to take a break. The day we decided that, we were in the cafeteria and Officer Hart was the resource officer at that time. At that time they had a substitute working Ben's place. Jerome started kidding around and told officer Hart that "Yeah, tomorrow you are going to be calling on *your* mind. " And Officer Hart said, "What are you talking about?" We never did tell him what our plan was, though. But that was our plan. We were just tired and worn out from breaking up fights, over doing our part in security work and not being listened to, essentially. It's a tiresome job after you get through. Some days you wake up with so many muscle aches and pains. And Ben had left us shorthanded in both experiences, manpower and muscle power. Tired and kind of disgusted, we just called in sick the next day. We didn't let Benny know.

So, I was at home relaxing, sitting around watching a video, when Ben called my house and said, "Floyd what's this going on at Central? I got a news flash saying they want to interview you because the security officers are on strike or something up at Central."

I found out they had a bunch of substitutes come there for just us five- Four, now. Now, all the students thought that we had quit, and they called their parents to go home. Parents were calling in to the attendance office and coming to pick up their children like hotcakes. I didn't know that we would affect the kids like that by not showing up for work one day! When we all showed back up the next day, Mr. Howard called us into his office and he asked us, "What is wrong!?" We just shrugged and asked him, "What do you mean?"

"You know exactly what I mean. You didn't show up for work yesterday. All of you called in sick at the same time. Now, what's wrong?" We said, "Nothing. We called in sick because we were sick and tired." We said, "It's not about a strike or making Mr. Johnson want to leave or anything like that."

We told him we had his back and we were back there now to work, etc., you know. That was the end of that. But we showed how much trust the student body had in us. By us not being there, they didn't feel safe without us. And the faculty or their parents definitely didn't want to trust any of the new security people. A lot of kids came up to us and said, "We were scared, man, because we thought you all had quit and left us." Some of them had gotten nervous and sneaked back home. "No, we reassured them, we just took a day off. That was all." They said O.K. then and got excited and started chattering because they were glad to see us back still working security. We weren't leaving them."

Jackie Fells: "It got to the place where the students, when we would write them up, they were not getting disciplined. Ben kept getting upset, but I kept telling Ben not to worry about it. If they don't do anything when we write them up, all we can do is leave them in the administrators' hands. When, not if, but when, something bad happened to one of those kids, it was on their head. But it seemed like the administrators didn't want to believe that some of these things were really going on in the school- that when we wrote the kids up, they were actually doing what we wrote them up about."

Floyd Smith: "It came to one point that this girl cursed Ben and Ben wrote her up about it. He told her she had to come with him to the office. She told Ben they're not going to do nothing to me, anyway. You can write me up and take me to the office, but I'll be back out here again. Ben wrote her up and took her down to the office. We looked up and the girl came right back out again and said, "See, I told you, you *so&so!#!...."and cursed him out again. Ben was getting really frustrated about some things, which I don't blame him. He decided that it was time for him to leave this school if he was in the position where the students could curse him out in the course of his duties and nothing be done about it."

Jerome: "Ben Johnson called a press conference. They came right out in front of the school and all the news media was there. He stepped out in front of the school and told them he was fed up with what was going on here. No discipline was going on at the school. Some of the students were jumping on other kids and students could curse him out when they felt like it. If we wrote them up, they would just get slapped on the wrist, like that.

In the beginning, it was like chaos and we had our hands tied behind our backs. The Vice Principal wasn't working with us every time we wrote the students up. I mean it was just one thing after another- like a knife in the back we had to deal with. We brought it to their attention several times. We said, "Look here, the students lack disciplinary action after we write them up." It was then that they told us downtown didn't want them suspending so many kids. We said we didn't care. If they jump on one, they got to go; if they curse us out, they got to go home for a break. They still didn't pay us any attention. So, Ben had a meeting with the press and resigned. He took his concerns downtown too."

Jackie Fells: "He and Say Macintosh started going downtown and showing up at the Board meetings to complain about the non-discipline that was going on at the school. He explained from his years of experience what was going on. They pretended to listen, but then, back at the school, it was the same old problems going on with the discipline. The word downtown was that they still didn't want that many suspensions. Every time that they would have a board meeting, Ben and Say Macintosh would show up every board meeting and complain anyway. Finally, Macintosh told Ben he could do more good at the school than not, and he thought he should just go on back to work. So Macintosh asked the superintendent if they had any problems with Ben continuing to work at Central. He said, No; that he would gladly take Ben back.

CHAPTER 34

Shorthanded

The next day, Ben came back to Central. Mr. Howard and Mr. Peterson didn't want Ben back over there. They saw him as a trouble maker for them. They told Ben to report to Mr. Bobby Jones. That is how I understand that Ben got transferred. They got a chance to get rid of Ben by transferring him over to Henderson Middle School. Now, the rest of us security who have been working with Ben for years were disrupted by this move. Administration decided they were going to hire some new ones. Principal Howard hired two new security officers. One was named Howard Love. Surprisingly, the other one was a female. I think her name was Robby (?)"

Floyd: "We were trying to break them in and teach them how the security office worked here at Central. Andrea, the female, would listen and try to learn from us how to do things properly. Love, he was a little different. He was a little hard headed-like he already knew it all and what to do. We soon found out that it would take more than two of them put together to make up for the loss of one Ben. We were really catching hell one day when a fight broke out. That manpower and experience that Ben would give us was definitely missing, and Jerry had also left for other employment. Jerome, Jackie and I were the only ones left out of the original five that had first started working as campus supervisors for Central High School. And we were severely handicapped."

Jackie Fells:" One day in the cafeteria, Howard Love tried to break up some girls from fighting, so we didn't think we needed to intervene with a female. But one girl just pushed him around forever. I mean, he wasn't nothing compared to what Ben would have done. And Robby was real young. She was almost the same age as some of the kids. She was learning from us, like I said, and she was a good student. But she couldn't control any fights and we needed instant help. Like I said, Howard Love didn't want nobody telling him what to do! He didn't even seem to want to learn how to work together. It was ridiculous how he got pushed around like that by a teenage girl. From my experience with him, he was always trying to find an easy way out. After that, they decided to hire one more lady to work with us. Her name was Andrea. She had been in the district for a while. She was real good because she was familiar with most of the kids and their families that came from the East end. She also knew a lot of the students around here dating back from her experience as a bus driver with the school district for five years. Andrea would also work with the department of Parks and Recreation Center during the summer months. So, she had a lot of experience. We were glad to have her with us because she had even more of the same experience and background than we had when we first got hired. She worked out real well on identifying students and members of gangs. She could talk to the kids very well. And she had their confidence to find out for all of us what was going on, or what some of the kids were planning to happen over the weekend. A lot of the problems would start up at different places over the weekend, and this she knew."

Floyd: "The year was going on and we would still have a whole variety of fights. We had been left with only three male security guards when a huge fight broke out in the cafeteria. I mean it was a bloody gang fight. So Jerome, Jackie and I really had to work out. Well, when the fight broke out, we started off by breaking them up in the cafeteria and trying to separate them out. We couldn't tell who all was involved because the kids kept running in and out. There were several kids originally involved in the fight and we had to break them up continually. More fighting broke out in the next hallway, so we started transferring whoever we thought might be involved up to the office. Then another fight would break out and we'd have to run down there and transport them up too. That day fights were breaking out like wild fire. We just didn't understand what was going on with these kids that day. It got to the point where a terrible fight broke out on the floor next to the main office. And these two guys in the fight were determined to kill each other! One of them pushed the other into the trophy case and broke the trophy case glass. At that time, I was upstairs transporting kids and had to call down to see if Jerome was still downstairs anywhere nearby. I ran back down there where the fight was going on. Glass was broken everywhere. When Ms. Smith yelled for Jerome, Jerome ran by and grabbed both the kids, risking his own life before 100- 150 lb. glass case fell on top of them. Jerome snatched them up and out just as the whole trophy case gave way.

We stopped everything and immediately transported these kids down to the nurse's office. One of their backs was cut up really bad. The other one- both of his wrists was cut up bad. An artery had been cut. Blood was every where all up and down Central's main hallway. There was so much blood that it looked like a battle zone. In hindsight, these kids would have been killed fighting each other if Jerome hadn't snatched them out from under that trophy case. At the time we transferred the kids to the emergency office, the chaos was still going on. Thankfully, by that time, officer Mosley had come in and called for extra city police backup officers to the school. Before we knew it, we saw this whole battalion of police officers quick stepping into the building. Even bicycle police pulled up. Police were on their way in and we security were on our way out. We had done all we could this time."

Jackie Fells: "The officers sprayed pepper spray in the building which ran everybody out of there; principal, vice principals, teachers, and security officers. They ran all of us up out of there. That same day, I think officer Mobley set a record in arrests. He arrested so many kids for fighting that we were already in his office packed with students he had arrested when he had to go out and make some more arrests. Like I said, I don't know what it was about this day, but it was one serious fight breaking out after another. Officer Mobley got to the point where he ran out of handcuffs. Other police officers gave him their handcuffs so he could continue with all the students he had to arrest. They called for more cars to take them down to the police station. This was the first time I gave serious thought to quitting. I started asking my friends around if they knew about any job openings."

CHAPTER 35

The Heat of the Moment

Floyd Smith: "One school morning early, we were all at our morning posts when one of the parents spotted a flame coming out of the auditorium. He called someone in the main office who then contacted security. They asked us to go to the auditorium and see what was going on. We called back and told them that the school was on fire. I was on 16th and Park Street at the time of the call and walked back to the campus toward the back of the school. I saw flames leaping out from the back of the school's auditorium. It appeared to be 20 or 30 feet high flames coming out from that window.

Someone from the main office hit the fire alarm outside the building. All the security officers ran like crazy inside the building and told the students to leave immediately, "You must leave the building!" We yelled it several times. Some of the teachers we told they needed to exit the building because the school was on fire wanted to wait because they had some things they needed to do. We told them, "No, there is not time." Unbelievably, we had to physically force some of these teachers out of the building! And I mean, smoke at that time was everywhere- smoking up the school. We ran from room to room making sure that the rooms were all cleared out. Then we went from the third floor down to the second floor informing students, teachers and all other personnel to immediately leave the building. We finally got the building cleared out by the time the fire department made it to the school. From the first fire truck that arrived, the fireman told me he needed me to run some hoses up inside the building and stop, grab the middle of it and run some more until he got enough hose up in there to fight the fire. I did that. Whew. I knew those hoses were pretty big, but they weigh more than you would think. Other fire trucks were starting to arrive by then. Five fire trucks came up on the campus. Very shortly thereafter, the firemen were fighting that fire for real. All the other Safety and Security Officers began to arrive. Together we rounded up the children around the school and moved them towards the gym area. Afterwards we called for the buses to return and pick up those kids who rode buses and take them back home.

The superintendent closed the school down for that day at Central. Multitudes of kids were around and all over the school grounds. Other people in the neighborhood found out about the fire and they started hanging around to watch. It became so chaotic with the smoke and flames, trucks and firemen, hoses, water, cars blowing their horns, etc., and kids were everywhere, not to mention the neighbors. But we managed to get our Central's kids into the gym. Fortunately, the buses arrived quickly and started picking them up. We monitored the ones who walked home and the ones that drove their cars; we hurried them on along to drive off. Then we passed the word out to the teachers and the rest of the staff that the school was closed for the day and they should leave. By the time we got all of them out and away from the campus, we looked up and it was close to four o'clock. It was time for us security to get out of there too. But we hung around for a little while longer in order to learn and see how we could help.

A lot of the firemen had had to abandon the building. The Red Cross came later and set up and provided cold water, food and coffee for everyone who was fighting that fire. I had an idea of a career change crossed my mind before I really saw how dangerous their job was also, and how hard they had to work all at once. You also needed to be in excellent physical condition. Some of the firemen became exhausted and stretched out and went to sleep out in front on the school lawn. Some of them still had to continue fighting the fire in relays while others had to come out and get some fresh air and rest. It was a huge fire. Later the next day, we found out that there were several hot spots. Someone had intentionally set the auditorium on fire."

Jackie Fells: "Well, the school was still smoking. They finally managed to put the fire out, but they had to get big fans to blow the smoke out of the building. While the fire department was fanning the smoke out of the building, we went inside and started looking around. All the power had been cut off. The fire chief had ordered the engineer to cut off all the electricity to the building so that the firemen could get in and out of the building safely. Bill called the principal and let him know that the fire chief had ordered him to cut off all power to the building. He was given the all clear before firemen took over the entire campus it seemed.

We got to talking to some of the administrators from security and they had a better way of doing what we did, of course. The worst they could come up with was that all the kids were still hanging around outside and why we couldn't move all those kids to another place? I told "judge" Evan that my priority was to get all the students out of the building, not to worry about where they were outside around the building. We were never given credit for the way we went into a burning, smoking building and cleared it out like we did. But, as for me personally; as long as I've been in the district and as long as I've been around in the world, I know we did under the circumstances, a very good job. Even the professional firemen had a time with that fire. We had gotten several hundreds of people out of an accelerated fire, burning, smoky building in time- even the ones who didn't want to leave, and didn't miss a one."

Jerome: "I found that very impolite for them to come and criticize, not giving us credit for getting all those children and teachers out in split second decisions at the time. Why didn't they do it then? Why didn't they go into a burning building and alarm the people with smoke all through it. That wasn't on my resume either. That was a huge task in itself using mind over matter. But it's no telling what you can do in emergency situations. Even though the kids were still around the school, they weren't rowdy or anything. They were just happy they were out of school and jumping around like it was a town party. Not only were other kids starting to show up, but people from all over the neighborhood started gathering around the school. So what could we do? They had to ask the city police to come and help keep the crowd away from the school, you know. The firefighters said we all did a good job, but that was one of the worst incidents I ever had to deal with under that type of pressure. You never know though what you are capable of doing until the heat of the moment, so to speak."

CHAPTER 36

You fire people who aren't doing a good job

Floyd: "For the new school year, we got our letter to report back for in-service training. We went for our first day of in-service training and found out that over the summer they had hired someone else as a mobile unit. This was a promotional job and we hadn't received any information about it. So we complained to Bobby Jones and asked him why we didn't get a chance at the promotional jobs. They hired this one guy named Benny McDonald as a mobile unit and he conducted a conference speech in one of our classes. He would always try to criticize us-even during the training in front of all the other security officers. I had had enough and I got up and said if they couldn't speak well of our security at Central in front of everybody, then they should not say anything at all about us.

They didn't understand our system and how we had to work things at Central. We go through twice the problematic situations and incidents in one day than <u>any</u> of them. And why was it that every time they brought in someone new, they always ended up having to ask us what to do and they didn't last. We had now been working for years and none of us original 5 had ever been fired. You fire people who aren't doing a good job, don't you?

For some reason, they just didn't want to give us any credit for what we did. Something was going on wrong. Even at the awards ceremony at Parkview High School where they gave superintendent awards; all the Resource officers and the Security Officers come to the awards assembly. One of the police officers came over to talk to me. He was disturbed and asked me, "Floyd, why is it all these other people are getting awards for doing less work than you all do. And you all didn't get any?" I say this is how they are now treating us as some kind of punishment. No matter how hard we work or how hazardous our duty was over at Central, they just don't give us that kind of respect. I have my suspicions as to why, but I don't know why. I joined a union and I can re-negotiate our contract. Maybe I didn't speak up when I should have and maybe because we spoke up too much about things that were not right. But somehow, we would now constantly being ridiculed by those with less experience than we have."

CHAPTER 37

Out to Lunch and AWOL

Floyd: "Well, we got through that in-service and start with the new school year. This season, I was placed over at the student parking lot. During lunch time, I still find that it is a majority of the white kids who are trying to leave the campus for lunch. I would constantly have to turn them back around since our campus is now closed. It got to the point where I had to hide around in the parking lot in order to see which ones were trying to leave. This one high-blond haired girl in particular, who drove a white BMW would always be the first one out of the building trying to leave. So one day, I decided to park my car over by her car. I'm over there in my car and here she comes again-running. She doesn't see me and thinks she's got a break, so she starts running like she's running for her life towards her car. I just pop out and politely say, "So where are we going?" She hollered and said, "Ooh you scared me." I said, "Yes. You need to turn yourself around and go on back to the campus. You know you're not supposed to leave the grounds for lunch." I could tell she was mad, but she kind of chuckled and went on back toward the school. But here we go again on the very next day. Here she comes out the door at the 14th Street exit this time. First she just looked around a couple of times. I was ahead at the parking lot and saw her looking all around to see if she could locate me. I just waited again and hid myself from her view in the parking lot. When she thought it was safe, she raced across the street. She had gotten about half way across the street when I popped up. She jumped and said, "You scared me!!", again. I said, "Girl, you need to just quit trying to leave the campus!" She was a senior and I found out she was trying to leave the campus to go and have lunch with her fiancé. I understood, but I just couldn't let her go because it is against school policy now to let a student leave the campus during the day for any reason without a permit. I had to turn that same girl around each and every day that I caught her.

This other incident that happened during Halloween was a situation where some girls were trying to leave the campus by way of the lower lot where the old tennis courts were. I saw them coming and decided to have some fun. These three girls were coming fast, and I hid from them. I had already taken a Halloween mask from another young guy earlier, so I put it over my head and stooped down in back of the truck. They thought they were home free and were jogging fast when I jumped out and scared the daylights out of them! I snatched the mask off and said, "It's just security officer Floyd. You don't have to be scared or anything, but where are you all going?" "Oh, uh, uh, no, we're not going anywhere." "That's right. I believe you. You all are not going anywhere." So I turned them around and sent them back to the campus. It sure was funny, but I had to compose myself until they were out of sight. Then I thought about the hyena.

We had a lot of students, mostly white students, but not just all of them, try to sneak off campus on that side. I started having to be very tricky about how I stopped them. I usually liked to be standing where they could see me and just turn around, but sometimes that wasn't possible. When they'd see me, they would run and jump in their car and speed off the parking lot and I couldn't run as fast as some of them anymore.

This year, the problem we started having was bad. A few of our students had slipped away from campus and had automobile accidents, not to mention the ones that played hooky and didn't return or returned intoxicated. I was working on that side, so I started locking the gate to keep them from going off if I wasn't there. That way I could just take my time and come around the side where a bunch of students would be sitting in their cars stalled at the gate trying to get out. They didn't know that I had locked it until they had driven the car around to the street gate. Then I would warn them that, "I'm not going to continue running you all down. I'm just going to have to start writing you up to get you to see the point that you cannot leave the campus during lunch period." So they would go park their cars, grouchy, some of them muttering bad words because they don't understand why they can't leave the campus, get something to eat where they wanted and come on back, etc. I would say, "Hey, I only enforce the rules, I don't make them." They would all just go on and re-park their cars.

But every day it would be the same old thing. They still keep checking me out to see if they can beat the old man and get off campus. I was around in my mid- thirties then, but I know how they were thinking. Some of them got smart and started parking their cars on the other side of the building on 16th street away from my side. That's how they started leaving campus from that side of the street. But hey, I couldn't be in two places at once. So, I put that action to a halt. I had to start locking all three parking lot gates. It slowed the running off campus problem down, but it created another problem on that side of the school. The kids started parking their cars on the streets, in front of peoples driveways and on neighborhood curbs. Ha. I guess where there is a will, there's a way.

Half way through lunch, I got called in one day and was told that we had problems in the lunch areas with kids who were at the picnic tables smoking. Teenagers used to be able to smoke at Central, but after everyone learned how unhealthy it was, smoking had been banned on campus. Jackie called me in to go inside the building and watch and see who these kids were that were out there smoking. The teachers were complaining that when they walked through the campus, they observed students sitting on the picnic tables, smoking right out in the open. I went up to the third floor where they couldn't see me, and watched them through a window. When I saw someone smoking, I called downstairs security and that student would be busted. We would do this every day. And each day during lunch period, they'd start the same thing: smoking. The kids would saunter off to the picnic area, take out a cigarette, light it up and continue to smoke in that area. It got to the point they started going behind the school and crouching down to their knees with the cigarettes. I had always heard that cigarette smoking is a difficult habit to break and I believe it. I'm glad I never started because we had to really concentrate on watching those kids in order to try to break up all that smoking.

While we try to solve the smoking problem, which we didn't have much luck with, we still have so many gang members inside the school. Most of the gang members would eat and hang out with each other inside the cafeteria and in the hallways right outside the cafeteria. So, we saw a problem we always had to deal with. We'd spend a lot of time trying to solve this, and then we would run back and try to solve the smoking problem. Over at the ROTC area, I smelled another kind of weed burning. Some of our students also liked to smoke the marijuana cigarette. I told them they had to stop that for sure because if I had to write them up for that, the consequences would be too serious. We'd try to go through and check all that out first- the campus lunch AWOL, parking, and the picnic and ROTC smoking- because at the end of the lunch period, we already know, is when the majority of the vicious fights broke out.

By the end of the lunch period, we would have come in closer and closer toward the cafeteria in order to keep an eye on the gangs. One gang in particular always had problems with other gang members. We always had to watch the East End gangs very closely. Our toughest fights would be East End versus someone else. A lot of them were bitter, mean and angry or I think, depressed. I don't know. But, we had to constantly keep our eyes on them. We'd tell the people in the cafeteria if they felt something brewing, don't hesitate to get on the radio and ask for back up way ahead of time, before they could get started well. That way we could all get to that area in time. If they saw all of the security guards there in the cafeteria, most of the time, they would not start to fight. But as soon as they could get in an area where there wasn't much security, that's when all hell would break loose.

So it was with one lunch period and some East Enders. We had a fight break out right at first door south. Some young men were following another one around and he said this was disturbing him. So, when he got a chance, the boy asked them, "What are you looking at?"

The way he told it, they just hauled off and punched him. They might not have liked the way he looked, what he had on, what he said, etc. You never know for sure. That's just the way the East End gang worked. Some of them, I'm sure had mental problems; they would just punch people for no reason.

CHAPTER 38

You can improve on the wheel, but you can't remake it

When Benny moved on to another school, Principal Howard needed another security officer in the cafeteria. He put a few more classroom teachers in the cafeteria to help us out. One of the teachers was a communications teacher by the name of Blackmon. I didn't think it was such a great idea to put Mr. Blackmon in there. He didn't have the character or the physique for that type of job. We explained to Mr. Blackmon how the kids would throw trays or ice down on the floor in front of you when a fight broke out, so he should be very careful how he approached any fights.

Lunchtime and another fight broke out. We got a call on the radio that a fight had broken out in the cafeteria. I was down on the south patio area at the time. As I came running in the south cafeteria door approaching where the fight was going on, I saw Mr. Blackmon rushing over there straight ahead to the fight. I immediately spied this kid who was sitting at one of the lunch tables when he tossed his tray on the floor right in front of Mr. Blackmon. A cup with ice in it was also thrown out in front of him.

Too late! Mr. Blackmon flipped up in the air, feet first, spinning around. I mean it looked like he was on a trampoline. I'll never forget it when all of a sudden he hit that floor-wham! But I had to continue quickly on to the fight. The little "angel"- because I shouldn't say what I really thought of him-tried to do the same thing to me. What I had to do was pass Mr. Blackmon on up, who was laying sprawled out on the floor looking stunned. I jumped up on the table right in front of the kid who had dumped his tray and purposefully, I stomped right up on him, as close as I could to him without stepping on him before I ran from there across the table, jumped onto another table; from table to table. That is how I made it over to where the fight was going on. I dived into the middle of the crowd and busted them up. I had to move bodies out of the way until I got to those kids who were fighting.

One of the running backs of the football team was eating his lunch and watching the fight when I accidentally knocked his lunch tray out of his hand while making it to the fight. By that time Simms and Fells came on in there and we grabbed the people who were involved in the fight. We broke them apart and transferred them up to the vice-principal's office. We walked upstairs to the area and separated them and gave them to the vice-principal individually.

On my way back down to the cafeteria, the football player approached me and said, "Man, You knocked my lunch right out of my hand." I told him I didn't mean to and gave him the money to buy another lunch. I was returning to check on Mr. Blackmon. By that time, the nurse's assistants had gotten him up and they were working with him because he was pretty bad hurt. He was sitting down and by the look on his face; we could see that he was in great pain from the fall. I was embarrassed because at the time, it had been funny to us. Not the fact that he had gotten so hurt, but the way he fell looked like he was on a trampoline. We transferred him up to the nurse's office so they could look at his injuries and see if his back was alright. Around that time, Mr. Blackmon being injured like that and this continuous terrible fighting were the main things that happened that were troublesome.

With Benny transferred to a new school, it was only Jerome, Jackie and me left to break up all these fights, which placed us under a lot of stress. And all the other people who were working with us, we'd teach them what were going on. New security officers or school teachers were being sent to us every other week it seemed. We would have to train them and work with them at the same time. We thought they were listening to us, but when they'd get hurt, we saw that they weren't listening to us at all. We tried to explain to them the reasons why we would tell them things so that no one would get hurt. This was another result of not listening to us about what would happen in the cafeteria when a fight broke out. We've all had some college classes, but I don't care if you are a college graduate and don't have the experience for the job, you should listen.

CHAPTER 39

FYI

We were at a football game over at Farrell working with our new resource officer. He was still fresh at the job and it was a Central High game vs. J Farrell. We were on the visitor's side and suddenly a group of kids arrived that didn't look like any of our kids. I decided that they must be from J. Farrell. They were a group of kids coming from the home team side back and forth to our side to visit. By the time the kids made it around to us and the new resource officer, I could tell he was fresh. When the kids came around and were directly behind us, he jumped and turned around to face them like he was surprised that they had the nerve to come around us to visit. Like I said, we were working with a new resource officer and we were shorthanded without Jerry Smith and Benny Johnson being with us anymore. Jerry had been put off by the blood and the fire and had also taken another job working for the railroad

You can not show a bad attitude or fear when you are working the gangs because they will see that attitude and feel you don't know your job. An attitude toward them is also an instigator for trouble. That is what I noticed about this officer. He was too uneasy around a group of kids when you have to let them know that you are the one in control. I wanted to tell the resource officer and ask him about that, but most of them don't want us giving them advice anyway. So I don't give them advice anymore. I started letting them learn on their own. I guess it is because they are officers that went through their police training and they only listen to other officers. But we have to work with these kids and we're in a school environment. It's not like we're in a city street environment.

For example, the resource officer had made an arrest of one of the kids that was fighting. One of the resource officers put the kid in handcuffs. He did not ask one of our security officers how to make an arrest with kids. He was in his office and turned his back for a spell or so. Before we knew it, we heard that the kid had broken out running. I was stationed on the north end when I got a call on the radio about this young guy who was running from the police. I saw him sprinting toward the 14th Street exit like a cheetah. I tried to run to that door and meet him there, but before I could get there, I saw the kid running away from the campus with handcuffs on. He dashed across the street and into somebody's back yard and I haven't seen him since. It wasn't even 3 minutes before we had officers surrounding the block and a helicopter. But, somehow, this kid managed to evade all those police officers and the helicopter. The guy had put his legs up and his arms over, reverted the handcuffs right in front of the officer and got away. I could have told him you have to watch our kids because they are faster, strong, and smarter than you think.

So we were still having a huge number of fighting incidents at the school. Mostly it was neighborhood against neighborhood. The majority of these guys are gang members from one neighborhood fighting members of a gang from another rival neighborhood or territory. For instance, one afternoon after the school let out, huge numbers of people were out there fighting; all of them standing up for the gang member turf in their neighborhood. It's crazy and ridiculous, but that is what's going on. They claim the rights to the streets, girls, houses, dogs, drug sales, air, etc. in their neighborhood. The resource officer, by the time he made it out there, got in the middle of it. We had to physically restrain all the people involved in it on the south side of the school. It was a furious fight. We really had to use super physical force to restrain them that time. When we finally got them broken up and everyone separated, we were escorting them up to the principal's office when one of the resource officers asked all excited, "Have any of you seen my gun clip?" Aw man, he lost one of his clips. We had to stop and immediately start searching for it because we sure didn't want any kids to have that. It was late, but we couldn't let anyone get his bullet clip to his gun. But we never did find that. We searched frantically several times and asked around, but we never did come up with it.

The new security officers had started taking off during basketball season. Jackie Fells was very upset about that. He started writing them up because they were forcing Jackie, Jerome and me to work harder. These other guys think they can get the job and just work in the mornings when they feel like it and skip basketball and foot ball season. When they did this, Jackie, Jerome and I would have to work harder and also make up for those overtime hours, which we were already working more than our share.

CHAPTER 40

Girls Gone Gang?

"On this particular early morning, on my side on Sixteenth Street by QT, the buses are pulling in and dropping kids off. There are always a lot of Crips members hanging out over there by QTs, so we keep an eye on them. It was getting close to time for the kids to be getting in and into their classrooms when I noticed this boyfriend and girlfriend coming around the corner toward 16th Street and they seemed to be upset. She reached over to him and and snatched a necklace off from around her boyfriend's neck. He grabbed her and slung her down on the ground, got on top of her and actually started to punch her. I hollered over there to him and told him to stop. He went on and punched her, and that's when I ran over there. I called on the radio a code 3 (a fight) around there, but nobody was there to answer, so I had to dive because he was steadily punching the young lady. I caught him with a forearm to the chest because I was trying to get there before he could punch her in the eye or something and really hurt her. I caught him in the chest with my elbow and kinda hit him too, I guess, and knocked him off of her. She was laying down on the ground crying. By that time Jerome made it outside around to where we were and I had the boy under control.

As we were taking the two upstairs, the Crip guys that were walking on Park Street toward 14th street around Qts said, "So, that guy likes to hit on girls, let us take care of him." I told those guys that he'd be taken care of and they just needed to move on. I had also avoided a serious incident because in spite of some of the things they do, the Crip guys do not respect men who beat up women. Jerome and I escorted both of them up to the vice principal's office. I wrote them up and let the vice principal deal with them. Jerome was talking to some of the kids and asking them what had happened. They were telling some of the kids that the way I had to jump, it looked like Floyd flew over there and knocked the boy off that girl. He started messing with me about that. We started laughing about how this job had turned me into Superman; the way I had to fly through the air in a single bound to stop the boy from beating on that girl.

The changes in some of the incidents we started having this year was girl friend and boyfriend fights. They would be serious like they were really married to that person. This one young lady was having it out with some other females at the school. We started having a lot of that between females again. We got a call from the second floor south in room 208 that girls were around there fighting. We all rushed over there where this short stocky young lady was fighting a tall slim one this time. Even as we were approaching them, the two were continuing to fight. The tall thinner young lady had a pipe wrench in her hand that she had used to hit the girl onside of her head. These two young ladies are still in a furious fight. The other young lady is swinging a pipe wrench at the stocky young lady and she was swinging back at her, just fighting her furiously like wrestlers on T.V. We rushed them to get between those two. One security officer grabbed long tall bright skinned and I grabbed the chunky brown one who was really trying to get at the other young lady. While she's trying to continue to fight her, she's hollering bad words and "that this bitch hit me upside the head with this wrench, I'm gonna kill her!" So we got them separated easily and we're trying to cool them down, but she's steadily trying to get the tall one. I believe this time she really wants to kill her, so we got long tall out of her sight. Then we rushed the other young lady out of the area so she can cool down from this incident. She was crazy with rage. We were finally able to escort the first one around to the principal's office. In this case, we had to escort the short one to the nurse so the nurse can check her out. She had been hit on the head with a wrench and we thought she might be threatening a heart attack. The nurse checked her out and thankfully she hadn't been seriously injured. The vice-principal did her job and suspended both of the young "ladies".

It wasn't but a few days later on Central's other end that we get a call for 4 girls fighting. We are trying to figure out what is going on. All of a sudden all these girls are fighting. We find out that these girls who are fighting; there is some relationship with them. And oh, Lord, we find out there is an East End girl's gang going on now inside of the school. They're having it out with some other girls. The other girls, I don't believe are related to the gangs, but they are friends who hang together. We have another epidemic of gang fights, but this is a change: Gangs of girls fighting other girls. It was another furious fight on the second floor. Someone told us that one of the girls had a box cutter. We ran up there and broke them up. One of the female security officers searched one of the females who had the box cutter. The teachers said they saw it, but we couldn't figure out where this girl had put the box cutter. We didn't see her pass it to anyone and we never did get a hold to it.

Another day comes, and I mean it hadn't been a day before we are having another girl fight. This time it's two sisters whipping up on a guy in the classroom. He's a pretty big guy too, wearing an ROTC uniform. One of these sisters is a big one. She is related to one of the secretaries in our school. When Jerome and I get in the room, we have to move chairs out the way to get to her. We looked to our right at the big girl. The principal is trying to hold her and looks like he is in a fight for his life. He was sweating, eyes all popped out, barely able to hold this girl down. I don't know, maybe that's how we looked to them sometimes. Anyway, Jerome went over and grabbed her and wrestled her on out of there. By this time, I had grabbed the young man. Some of the other students had helped us and held the slimmer girl down. As I'm taking the boy down to the office, I look at his head. The poor guy has got knots all upside his face and head. His shirt had the buttons torn off. Those two girls had done a number on him. So we took him to the nurse's office first and had the nurse to check him out. The other security officer escorted the other young lady out. These girls were just out of control. They said they heard that someone said the boy had said something about them, so they beat him up like that. He say, she say. The vice-principal dealt with it. At the end of that day, they ended up going home for a short vacation."

CHAPTER 41

Demons at the School

I can remember one morning, Jerome, who is very religious, asked us all to come together inside the auditorium. The security police all held hands and started to pray. Jerome says he feels some bad demons inside the school of Central High now. He feels we need to start praying in order to overcome these legions of demons. So we came together and started praying every morning. We'd pray to God for a while and everybody would feel like; "Now, we're ready to go and do our job."

Okay, so right after we did this early one morning, we noticed some girls coming, running out of the restroom. They ran straight up to the security and started yelling, "He's in there. He's in there!" We said, "Who's in there?" "A man came in the girl's restroom." We rushed in there and started looking and didn't see anyone. We said, "Where is he?" They said, "That is him." We encountered this attractive looking girl wearing a mini-skirt. She had her hair slicked back in a strange fashion though. This..., I mean, it looked like a young girl to me- had breasts like a female. I mean he looked like a young woman. But, they said, "No! He's not. He's not a female, he's a male. He's just dressed like that."

Amazed with confusion, we decided to take their word and told him, "You have no business in the girl's restroom. You have to go to the boy's restroom." He refused, so we took him in to the principal. They started talking to him and trying to get him to change his ways and use the boy's restroom. But he said, "No way." He said that he was not going into the boy's restroom. We told him he could not go into the girl's restroom because the girls did not feel comfortable with him in there; a young man dressed up like a female. So they came to a decision about him. The nurse said for him to start using the restroom in the nurses office because this kid said he was never going to use the boys restroom, which really I don't blame him. There's no telling what those guys would have done to him if he came in on them dressed up like that.

And after Jerome prayed, we started seeing these strange activities.

We began to notice more of a separation between the resource officers and security officers. The resource officers seemed to want us to work under them instead of with them. Jordan, who was a good friend of mine, was one of the first resource officers we started working with. We were always able to work well with him. But we could feel the separation widening between some of the newer resource officers and us. I remember how I once called a resource officer several times on the radio when I really needed him. For the first time in my career, no one responded. When I told him later and asked him if he had heard my call on the radio, he said, "Well, what did you need!?" I mean some of them were really getting obstinate. And I also understand they were becoming like that with some of the children. I mean, it felt like we were working against each other instead of together. Several times we called on him and could not get an answer like a chilly ghost at the other end. I started realizing not to depend on them when I needed assistance in any situation.

Its summertime and time for us to have our in-service training review again and that's when it all came out. The resource officers all come there to Central and I notice they seem to be very upset with us security officers. One of them got up there and suddenly made a threat. Right now today, I don't understand why he said what he said; "When you tell it on me, I'm gonna tell it on you!". I thought about what Jerome had said. This officer had changed his attitude like a negative spirit overtaking him. He had been falsely informed about the old H. era. He never did explain that, though- why he said what he did. That is why we became so divided, I guess. That old problem about H. was still rearing its ugly head. We started pulling apart from each other and became them and us, when in the past we had always worked together. But now they have added some new younger ones treating us snobbishly while I have had more than twelve years in the business of high school security. Most of them haven't even been officers, so I don't understand them attempting to separate themselves from us. Knowing what I do, if we don't work together, it will be hard to keep the school under control. But I don't say too much to any one of them. I speak to them on a regular basis, but when it comes to why they are distancing themselves from us, I don't question them anymore. Evidently they have their own priorities and they don't tell us, so we move on ahead.

CHAPTER 42

Training the Trainers

We have the fortieth anniversary for the Little Rock nine coming up next year. Maybe that is what everyone is all straight lipped about. It's hard to believe it has been 30 years since I first sat in the auditorium here at Little Rock Central High and watched that Christmas ballet. Bobby talked to Jackie about putting the security together perfectly. The President's secret service come here and begins to meet with Jackie in order to work out all the details about how our security will be done.

During our in-service, we noticed that one of the guys dressed up for this new security firm used to be a security officer over at Dunbar Jr. High. So the other guys said, "Isn't that the security guard who used to work over at Dunbar *Junior* High School?" He said, "Yeah, yeah. He has his own security firm now." So we started chatting with him and he said that one day we're going to be working for him. He indicated that he and Bobby Jones are going to be part owners in his new security firm. After talking to him for a while, he began his demonstrations. He brought out some security people who worked for him and they are going to teach us self-defense. We chuckled when we noticed immediately that he didn't know what was going on. He brought in these small, short, and a weasel looking guy dressed up all neat and shiny in security uniforms. They demonstrated how to restrain and remove a kid that was s sitting in a chair. Wow! I wish. But, O.K., we had some questions and just for the devil got in Jerome:

"Why would you need to use pressure points on a kid who is sitting in a chair?"

"Because you asked him to move and he would not follow your orders."

"But at this point he is not a threat to anyone. He is just sitting in a chair. So let the kid sit in the chair, you know, and remove the other kid from the room."

"Why don't you just knock him out and drag him where you want him?"

Anyway they continued to teach us their way. We had already realized these guys had never worked security inside a school. We could not do what they were trying to teach us to do with children. But anyway we kind of laugh and got a joke out of these security guys trying to teach us how to restrain children in chairs. Needless to say, we were not that popular in this meeting. Most of us have been doing this for a long time and we already know what to do, but we did want to learn any useful new scenarios. So we said, "O.K. show us how you go into a fight. I mean, a real fight." They proceeded to demonstrate. Well, a lot of kids, especially if it's a gang fight, they would have their mates to lock their arms up together and make a chain around the combatants in order to keep the security guards from getting to the fight. But, we had to get in there. We found it necessary to be real physical in order to get in there and break the chain links of young men they would make to prevent us from getting to the incident. We imitated a chain link for them and asked those guys how they thought better to do something in order to get through it and break up a fight. Well, they had never seen anything like this before and they just couldn't do it. They said, "Well, if they're really doing that, then someone needs to go to jail!"

Well, duh....if they're *really* doing that, that is the way our job would work and we had to deal with it. There is no way we were not going to make it through to that fight. Someone could get killed. *Hell*, No. We are not going to let no kids create a chain link locked up to prevent us from getting in there!! "If you all want to teach us how to better handle our situation, then we ask that you come up here and work our situation sometime to see what we have to deal with." We learned nothing useful from that security guard team. They went to Bobby Jones and complained that we were impolite and they did not want to come back and train us anymore. I was glad that they did not want to come back and waste our time because they could not relate to us with what we have to go through. Anything less than that couldn't help us out.

CHAPTER 43

From the Beginning and the End

O.K. now, in-service training is over with. It's time this year, 1997 School year and we are getting ready for an important anniversary. It's supposed to be a huge affair. News media from all over the world are here. President Clinton is going to speak, the Governor, the Mayor, and several major dignitaries. A black female president of Central High school will be speaking also. And the famous Little Rock Nine are coming from all over the United States. Secret service men are milling around over at the park. They're checking it all out this year. They are digging and dumping and cleaning the place up real well. People from the neighborhood are coming in to help and putting up big posters down stairs in the big patio area in front of the school. I mean, it's a huge event. They begin building over to the north end area in front of the school. They built up a big stage in that area for the media, and a place to handle their cameras and equipment. We import speakers the size of a small house and a large ramp area was built for the handicapped wheelchairs. We got it, you name it. The street is now blocked off in front of the school.

So we security get our details early one morning. This is the morning before someone from the secret service will explain to everyone what is going to go on at the event. At the time, we met a secret service lady, who was dressed real nice. She said she would like to have us inside of the building. I did not want to show up on the day of the commemoration affair because I thought with the entire President's secret service agents, there's going to be more than enough security to handle any situation. And as the day goes on, more and more secret service men start to show up. We met with the nice, attractive secret service lady on a regular basis that day. So far it's been a good day; no fights, no kids with serious incidents. Everybody is behaving themselves and making a perfect impression for our guests.

At the end of the day, a man who told us his name was just Jack gave us our details. We're told to meet with the Director of Security down at the football stadium and get our job descriptions. Well, I thought that we were supposed to be inside, but that had changed because the principal, Ms. Russo, told them she thought our people should be outside with the crowd rather than inside the school building. Ms. Russo also made the decision for the other vice- principal to be outside, which we thought was kind of strange. We thought the vice- principal would be there with the principal on the inside of the building. But evidently that is what she and Mr. Howard decided. Everyone would remain outside with the public. They would be the only two people inside with the President and the other two dignitaries to give their full attention.

So this morning we met down at the football stadium with Bobby Jones and his team in order for them to get specific details of our assignments. After we got our details, Jackie told us that we were not to go inside that building. Secret service men were all over and inside the school buildings. Anyone who was not a dignitary that had been pre-screened would no longer be allowed to go in there.

People are starting to walk towards 14th Street. Its called Daisy Bates Drive now after the activist who had a major effect on the Little Rock Nine's integration into Central High. We went up to the front where we were given precise instructions on where Central's security guards are to station. Before we can get to our locations, some Washington D.C policemen searched everybody who came inside to see the President. A tent had been set up for him with the Little Rock policemen stationed all around it. City buses had been parked up in a line in rows in the back and also school buses were parked in a row down a line on Park Street. This was part of the Secret Service's detail in order to prevent assassination attempts.

No one had seen Howard Love, one of our security team members. Then the secret service contacted Jackie Fells, our supervisor now, and told him how Howard Love had taken his key and gone on inside the building. Apparently, he had been too lazy to walk around the school building like everybody else. He had defied Jackie who told us repeatedly <u>not</u> to go inside that building; but he went anyway. The secret service guys jacked him up! Whatever they had done, right now to this day, we don't know because Love never would tell us exactly what happened when he went inside the building. The secret service men turned him over to Jackie, and Love wouldn't speak. But, they told Jackie they think they scared the living daylights out of him and he might need to go home for a while and wash up.

Suddenly, we heard the sound of the Presidents' motorcade. The ambulance siren, you could hear motorcycles, you could hear all those high-polished cars trailing by. We looked up on top of the buildings and saw secret servicemen standing using telescopes and binoculars to overlook the entire area. Look to the right and you could see several secret service men on the very tops of the school buildings. You look over to the left and you saw two other guys with huge binoculars who are overseeing everything.

And finally, our President Clinton makes it up the walkway into Central High School's building. When he gets inside, all of a sudden, they swing the doors open wide! And all of the Little Rock Nine start marching down the steps to the stage. As I remember, we had the governor and the mayor was up there on stage with our principal and the vice principal. Rudolph Howard came out with the Little Rock Nine, but the other vice principal stayed outside with us. Everyone was clapping and cheering like crazy. Then they finally started the presentations. The first person spoke and I remember it was Mr. Howard. He got through with his speech, but I have forgotten exactly what he said. The second person to speak was the president of the school, which was a female at that time who told how honored she was to be president of the school that used to wouldn't allow someone like her on the campus. A couple more people spoke.

I started looking around. It seemed like half the town was here. This was the biggest event Little Rock has ever seen since Bill Clinton became our President. We look around at the banners and signs and see people who came here from California, New York, Washington DC, Florida, Africa, Great Britain... from all over the world. Movie stars are here. You name it. They are all here at Little Rock Central High. Also, the vice president was up there on the stage with his wife. You could start looking around for all kinds of movie stars and famous people because they were there. Everybody came in to celebrate the fortieth anniversary of the Little Rock Nine's desegregation of Central High. The entire town came to a standstill and came to Central High to see this memorable event of our time.

As the commemoration was going on, some handicapped people started protesting and they got real loud. Jerome went over there to them- to the handicapped designated area where they were making all the noise. He held his hands up and asked them to quiet down. That didn't help, so Skip Rutherford, Clinton's assistant, walked over toward that way to see what was going on. I have never seen so many secret service agents show up. Secret service men came out of the woodwork. It seemed like there were almost as many secret service men as there were people there to see the event. They all walked over to the people who were protesting. I didn't hear it, but evidently Skip said something to them that made the handicapped people quiet down. After that, all those secret service guys started easing back inside the North end of the school.

The event took off. All the speakers got up on stage and made their speeches and presentations and all, while everybody was waiting for President Bill Clinton to speak. This is his home and everyone is real fond of him. I remember when I used to be up at the YMCA and Clinton would start jogging. He would jog up by the YMCA and he would always speak to me. Another thing I remember about him; that once he met you, he'd remember your name and never forget your face. Most of us respected him very much. He is an extremely intelligent man. Most people meet you one time wouldn't remember, meet you the second time, they might remember. But not Bill Clinton, he always remembered and said, "How you doing there, Floyd. How's it going?"

So the event continues to go on until finally our President Bill Clinton came up to the podium to speak. While everybody else was speaking, you could still hear talking in the crowd. But, when President Clinton got up to speak, you could hear a pin drop. He delivered one of his most powerful speeches about the Little Rock Nine. He named each and every one of them and called them all one by one, by their full names. He got to talking about the time in 1957 when African American children were not allowed to attend Central High School. Nine students took on that challenge. He castigated the governor at that time and said how wrong it was for him to deny those nine students the right to go to Central High School. I mean, it was one powerful speech that day! It was not too short and not too long. He was talking and when he got to the end of his speech, you did not want it to end. You wanted him to go on and tell us more historical information and his thoughts on the Central High crisis.

That is how powerful a speech it was for Little Rock in the State of Arkansas on the fortieth anniversary of the Little Rock Nine's return to Central High School. At the end of his speech, the whole convocation stood up and applauded and clapped on and on. They walked back up to the front entrance of the school and opened the door and continued to hold it open. President Clinton and the governor opened the doors themselves and invited the Little Rock Nine into Central High School, in contrast to what happened in 1957. Everyone was very emotional to see this sad part of American history. At that moment is when the Little Rock Nine all started walking through the door. Some of them were crying. I remember everybody looking up and around. Everybody looked at them and each other with such a proud smile, not thinking that something like that could ever have happened here at our school. They were overjoyed.

Now we have come to the point where any African American children are not allowed to attend any school anywhere in Arkansas. So that was an incredible moment for me and everyone else. Clinton said that we can go ahead now and move on. People were crying everywhere and I was really emotional myself. President Clinton left the stage and walked over toward the security's barricade where the people were hanging over the barricade. He started shaking everybody's hands with the secret service moving all around him. By the time he finished with the people there, he moved back toward the stage and went toward the building. As they walked to the building, the crowd parted in front of them as they went along;. President Clinton and the Little Rock Nine. You still hear people talking about what went on that day. I can proudly say that I was there during a historical moment such as this.

I did not want to be there working as a security officer during the commemoration ceremony. I knew there would be people there telling me what to do and where to be. I wanted to be able to hear all the speeches and what was being said because, especially when Clinton speaks, you listen.

We kept an eye on everything and had to help move everybody on. The crowd is getting a little thinner. Suddenly, we can hear the motorcade leaving from the back of the school, down the back way and out toward the freeway. He was gone. When our President left, we went around the school checking around for anything suspicious. Secret service guys were leaving out from the building carrying big cases of shoulder missiles. It was an event everyone here will remember. I believe it was kind of the final chapter to the Little Rock Nine crisis episode. Even after the Commemoration was all over, there were still a lot of affairs going on around town pertaining to it Like I say, it was an event that happened here at Central High like I had never witnessed before, just like that Nutcracker ballet thirty years ago when I had no idea what was going on.

Little Juanita is 79 years old now and has been retired for over 14 years. Her husband passed away 5 years ago on Christmas day. In addition to four of her children graduating from Central High; she has 3 grandchildren that also graduated from Little Rock Central. She still lives in the same house near Central High and loves to tell the story of the beautiful building that was built while she was walking to Capitol Hill Elementary School for Negro Children.

Conclusion:

The Castle Remains

Many people put their life on the line and sacrificed their dignity for the right to go to school at Central High. One of the Little Rock nine told how she had gotten separated from the rest of the group of pioneers and her dress was covered with spit from the racist mob there to prevent her from going to class. Now that black children have the ability to attend school anywhere in the state of Arkansas, too many of them just take it for granted and don't do their best to achieve. They have failed to appreciate and take advantage of the hard-won tools that have been provided for them to be successful adults.

When I began my career there as a campus supervisor, I did not believe what was really happening inside the walls of Central High. I had been very proud to attend this school as a teenager myself, and had worked hard to be accomplished here. As a product of an originally segregated school system, I had to re-ask the question because it did not appear that our children were better off now integrated.

Many of our parents had to worry about more serious things concerning equality than we did; like, not being able to attend any school at all. An elder related how despite her excellent grades, that as a black student, she would have had to leave the state in order to attend one of the few medical schools available to her. There are numerous stories about how white people, the Ku Klux Klan, etc. murdered and abused African Americans; and yet we had a sense of community and pride that seems to be lacking in kids today. Black children seem worse off now in this respect than we were. For the first time, to my knowledge, black kids are deliberately killing and abusing each other. They call each other vicious name. We see it every day.

I looked around and saw how many of the teachers are still disappointing in their prejudiced attitudes toward the children. Several members of the staff were not setting good examples of equal evaluation and fair play. Some of the examples were down right racist in nature. In addition, I hear stories of total lack of parental support in the home and serious family problems of disintegration involving drugs, alcohol, prison and sexual abuse.

I hope our kids will be able to overcome all these present obstacles in their lives. In spite of their circumstances, I hope they will continue on to be successful like the Little Rock Nine long after they leave Central High. However, there is not going to be a future unless they take care of the present, diligently, and get a decent education. They need to take advantage of the tools at the school provided regardless of their present situations so they can have a good life after they leave Central High; and move on and do bigger and better things. The Greek statues that represent Ambition, Personality, Opportunity and Preparation are still the keepers of "The Castle" and through the many decades things have changed but the "The Castle" has and always will remain constant.

Image 6